Amelia B. Johnson

**From Life's School to the Fathers House**

Amelia B. Johnson

**From Life's School to the Fathers House**

ISBN/EAN: 9783337027490

Printed in Europe, USA, Canada, Australia, Japan

Cover: Foto ©Andreas Hilbeck / pixelio.de

More available books at **www.hansebooks.com**

# FROM LIFE'S SCHOOL

TO

# THE "FATHER'S HOUSE."

## A brief Memoir and Letters

OF

## AMELIA, ANNIE, AND THOMAS JOHNSON,

### WIFE, DAUGHTER AND SON

OF

## JAMES JOHNSON

### COMMISSIONER OF CUSTOMS, CANADA.

COMPILED AND EDITED BY

## M. R. J.

## Toronto;

### HUNTER, ROSE & COMPANY.

### 1888.

# PREFACE.

---

THE life of a faithful servant of our Lord Jesus Christ can never fail to benefit those who come within its influence.

She whose letters follow the brief sketch of her life, here given, was one who lived a life of faith in the Son of God; who endured as seeing Him who is invisible; who, while in the world, was "kept from the evil."

Mrs. J. Johnson "departed this life in God's faith and fear," on the 24th of January, 1888. Her sorrowing family, in the hope that her example and words may be made, by God's blessing, a help and stimulus to some, as well as a comforting memorial to her friends, publish these simple details of her home life, and last illness.

> Farewell friends ! but not Farewell ;
> Where I am, ye too shall dwell ;
> I am gone before your face
> A moment's worth, a little space.
> When ye come where I have stepped,
> Ye will wonder that ye wept :
> Ye will know by true love taught,
> That *here* is all, and *there* is naught.
> Weep awhile if ye are fain ;
> Sunshine still must follow rain ;
> Only not at Death, for Death
> Now we know, is that first breath
> Which the souls draw when we enter
> Life, which is of all life centre.
> —ARABIC HYMN.

# FROM LIFE'S SCHOOL
## TO THE "FATHER'S HOUSE."

OTTAWA, Ont., Canada,
March 14th, 1888.

MY DEAR A.,

You ask for some particulars with regard to the life and the last days of our dear mother, who passed away seven weeks ago.

MOTHER! How we love to dwell on the word! How we love to recall the dear face; the smile of rare sweetness; the clear hazel eyes; the wavy brown hair which to the last showed scarce a thread of silver.

From our earliest childhood she was an inspiration to us. By precept and example she incited us to diligence, teaching us the nobleness of self-denial and the unworthiness of a life lived for self. To educate and improve every faculty to its utmost capacity, and to use these faculties so as to benefit others—"to be a blessing"—were the aims in life she held up before us. How many times has she held the childish, upturned faces between her hands and said, as she imprinted a kiss upon the brow, "The Lord bless you and make you a blessing."

While it was always her habit to "look well to the ways of her household," she was abundant in her labors for the suffering and sinful wherever it was her lot to dwell. Her thoughtfulness for others, and her industry, knew no bounds. Possessed of a rare degree of ingenuity, she never failed to discover some means of reaching those whom she wished to influence, from persons of refinement and culture down to the lowest outcast.

"You never give anybody up," a friend said to her one day, on hearing of the reformation in heart and life, through her efforts, of one who had been far gone in sin. And this was true: in the face of dissuasion, opposition, ridicule, she went out after the erring ones and strove to lead them to a new life.

During her married life her lot was cast in several different cities. In each of these, a lasting monument in the shape of some beneficent work set on foot by her, was left, to mark the fact that she had sojourned there.

She never went from a place without leaving it in some respects better through her influence, while her work for individuals, carried on so quietly that eternity alone will bring it to light, was unceasing.

She was wonderfully brave in sorrow, though naturally of an extremely sensitive, nervous temperament. She had a great deal of elasticity and sound common sense. Through and in and over all, her firm unwavering faith in an ever-present God sustained her in the most trying circumstances, and crushing bereavements. Her children will never know what she suffered in parting with four of them at one time, two sons being sent to a college in New York State, and two daughters to Mt. Holyoke Seminary in Mass. Whatever seemed to her to be for their highest good, must be done at whatever cost to her own feelings.

On three occasions during her lifetime God called her to give to Him a loved one from her circle of six, three boys and three girls. The first to be taken was a lovely infant of twenty months ; then, many years later, the eldest daughter, the pride of the family, just as she had completed her twenty-first year : four years elapsed, and then the eldest son, over whose career she watched with unusual solicitude, was called to join the sister whose loss he had never ceased to mourn with more than ordinary grief.

The following extract, from a letter written by her in 1883, will give an insight into the cheerful view she took of life, and her hope for the world. After alluding to some calamities which had recently taken place in different parts of the world, she adds :—

How delightful it would be to know that all these things indicate the speedy coming of our Lord ; coming to put things in order, to bring light out of darkness, order out of confusion ; to make an end of the works of the devil. It looks to me like expecting a great deal, to look forward to being taken to Heaven without dying; as so many do who are looking for the " coming." Now, though I can never make up my mind to accept the theories we have on this subject, nor understand the Bible statements concerning the end, still I hope on and ever *that it may be soon.* Not that I do not enjoy life as well as ever I did, indeed better I think ; I fear sometimes I love life and the blessings that are heaped upon me, too well, so that I am almost always filled with praise and thanksgiving, but there are so many reasons why we should desire the *new departure.* The wicked never will understand the folly of sin ; generation after generation, it is the old story of blindness and rebellion, and will be till the coming of the Lord. This, I think, the Bible plainly says. That,

however, should never discourage those who are working for their
fellows ; their work is with Him who says, " a cup of cold water
shall not lose its reward."

But perhaps we are not looking for the reward—well then, from
the same source we have, "Cast thy bread upon the waters and
thou shall find it after many days." "In due season we shall reap,
*if we faint not.*" Was it not strange (and the idea has just struck
me) that when the seventy returned to Jesus and told Him that
the devils were subject to them through His name. He said, "Rejoice not that the devils are subject unto you, but rather rejoice
because your names are written in Heaven." Now is it not the
case that we would be likely to rejoice more over the subjection of
the evil one, than at the fact that our names are written in Heaven ?
We do so want to see the kingdom of Satan overthrown, his awful
power over the children of men broken, his dens of iniquity destroy-
ed, his captives delivered, etc., etc. So we should, and I feel sure
that a God of love will find means to turn all Satan's plans, all
that he does, and all that he ever did to the furthering of His gracious designs of mercy to the children of men. I cannot help this
conviction.

Once in speaking to a friend of the work God had
given her to do, she said it was mainly in the direction of
"Gospel Temperance." Many through her intrumental-
ity were saved from lives of bondage to the fatal appetite for liquor, while her interest in the great work of the
Woman's Christian Temperance Union was intense. Of
this Miss Frances E. Willard, President of the National
W.C.T.U., writes as follows :

We have just received the beautiful, pitiful card and newspaper notice of your blessed mother's departure. Surely she was ripe
for Heaven ! But how sorely you will miss her.

Very clearly comes to my memory the good Bishop who called on
me summers ago at the White Mountains, and told me of the saint-
ly woman who had prayed that the white ribbon movement might
come to the Dominion capital, and he was so earnest that I agreed

to go when I had no such plan. Then I went with dear Anna Gordon, and was your guest twice. What solicitude your mother showed, how kind your father was, and how graciously the ladies rallied. Dear Heart ! She has gone home to her own native climate and companions. We work on in faith and hope.

From her family, who were privileged to watch with her night and day during her illness from New Year's morning until the twenty-fourth, the memory of that sacred season can never pass away. From the first she knew she was going home, and her one desire was to prepare us for it, her one thought was to comfort those she was leaving behind. For herself, she longed to go; her constant prayer was, "Oh take me," but to those whose hearts were breaking she had always some sweet word of comfort. " The Lord will sustain you," she would say ; or again, " you must think of it as a *Victory*, and do not mourn when I am gone." Once when she had said to one of us, " you do not expect me to recover now, do you ? " And the answer, through choking sobs, had been, " yes, darling mother, we all expect you to get well,"—she turned a little wearily and softly prayed, " O Lord, teach them better,"

Dear children," she said one day, " isn't it wonderful that we should have this experience."

She suffered much from difficulty of breathing and extreme weakness. It always comforted her to listen to words from Holy Scripture, repeated in her hearing by her ever attentive pastor, or her sorrowing family. On Saturday night, the 14th of January, she was wonderfully restful and filled with a peace and joy, not of earth, and lay so quietly; but whenever the hourly medicine was administered had some sweet, bright word to say to the son and daughter who were sitting up with her. Once she seized and kissed over and over again the hand of the latter, repeating many times the caressing words, "precious love, precious love."

At another time as she awoke from a short sleep we heard her repeating with much fervor, "Blessing, and honour, and glory, and power, be unto Him that sitteth upon the throne, and unto the Lamb forever and ever." Again, with her eyes fixed in an earnest gaze upward, she exclaimed, "Beautiful—heaven—God." These, and similar words, she repeated many times, always with her gaze upturned, and apparently quite unconscious of her earthly surroundings. Toward morning she began talking of a beautiful stream; "Oh the waters are sweet!" she said frequently; and, turning to her daughter with an earnest longing look, "Engulf me in the stream—you can, cannot you?"

About eight days before the end, she, with her family, partook of the Holy Communion. Though very weak, she was conscious of all that passed, repeated portions of the service aloud, and when at the close she was asked by the clergyman, "Have you any fear of death?" her reply was, "Oh, no; for years I have had no fear of death."

Although at times she would rally in a manner astonishing to her physicians and to those who were watching for her to breathe her last, the sad truth forced itself upon the minds of her daughters, who clung to hope in spite of the medical verdict, that the end could not be far off. Nine days before the end we watched without hope. These days were relieved by the sweet words that fell from her lips, sometimes with almost her old playfulness and sense of humor, but more often with a solemnity and tender affection which showed us that in almost every word she was taking leave of us. Those were days of desolation when every act performed, every little service rendered, seemed as if done for one who had already passed beyond the need of our loving care; when each familiar object seemed to look at us with a new, strange expression, as if reiterating to us our loss; when God seemed far away, and prayer a difficult, strange thing, and fierce temptations to doubt assailed us.

On the night of the 22nd, when hearing and speech had almost failed, the watchers at her bedside thought they caught from her lips the words, "O speak,—comfort."

Strength was given one of her daughters to repeat from the 14th of St. John, the words:—

"Let not your heart be troubled; ye believe in God, believe also in me.

"In my father's house are many mansions: if it were not so I would have told you. I go to prepare a place for you.

"And if I go and prepare a place for you I will come again and receive you unto myself: that where I am there ye may be also."

There she paused, thinking her mother did not hear. But a few moments after the stillness was broken, and the sweet, faint voice was heard distinctly to say, "Whither I go ye know and the way ye know—a full atonement made."

They were the last words uttered by her on earth; but the clear, expressive eye, and a faint gesture of the hand told the affection, and expressed the thanks for any little service rendered, which the lips were unable to utter.

After eighteen hours of unconsciousness, the spirit was released from the prison-house, and she went upward to her God.

Beautiful soul! God help us to live worthy of her, and give us grace to join her one bright day!

"He will swallow up death in VICTORY."

### HEAVEN.

Oh, what is this splendor that beams on me now,
    This beautiful sunrise that dawns on my soul,
While faint and far-off land and sea lie below,
    And under my feet the huge golden clouds roll?

To what mighty king doth this city belong,
    With its rich jewelled shrines, and its gardens of flowers;
With its breaths of sweet incense, its measures of song,
    And the light that is gilding its numberless towers?

See! forth from the gates, like a bridal array,
    Come the princes of heaven, how bravely they shine!
'Tis to welcome the stranger, to show me the way,
    And to tell me that all I see round me is mine.

There are millions of saints, in their ranks and degrees,
    And each with a beauty and crown of his own;
And there, far outnumbering the sands of the seas,
    The bright rings of angels encircle the throne.

And oh if the exiles of earth could but win
   One sight of the beauty of Jesus above,
From that hour they would cease to be able to sin,
   And earth would be heaven ; for heaven is love.

But words may not tell of the vision of peace,
   With its worshipful seeming, its marvellous fires ;
Where the soul is at large, where its sorrows all cease,
   And the gift has outbidden its boldest desires.

\*     \*     \*     \*     \*     \*     \*

Because I served Thee, were life's pleasures all lost ?
   Was it gloom, pain, or blood, that won heaven for me ?
Oh no !   one enjoyment alone could life boast,
   And that, dearest Lord ! was my service of Thee.

FABER.

## II.

It was our mother's habit to write to her absent children twice a week, and the following letters are selected from hundreds, of a similar nature, as being an index to her loving, helpful, energetic character, and as containing advice too valuable to be limited to the eyes for which alone it was at first intended. They are arranged without any regard to chronological order, as the good counsel they contain is applicable to all times and circumstances.

Most of these which are here given were written to her eldest son, shortly after he had commenced his labors as a clergyman at the age of twenty-three.

She always encouraged her children to write in the most unrestrained manner to her, and she was the confidante of all their joys and sorrows; she shared in their various exercises of mind, and was appealed to for help in every trouble or perplexity; help which was never wanting, and which never failed to dispel discouragement or anxiety:

" FREDERICTON, 20th May, 1867.

" MY VERY DEAR SON :—

" I have just received and perused with much pleasure yours of the 7th inst.  It is so gratifying to hear all about your circumstances and your feelings.  You cannot be too circumstantial in these things.

"I suppose you will have to suffer with weakness and timidity to some extent for a long time, yet, as you say, if you were more completely given up to God perhaps you would feel less solicitude.  Now you must examine your heart carefully and find out which gives you most uneasiness, the fear of not being a blessing to the people, or the fear of appearing to disadvantage yourself.  Try to get the matter settled, and expect that our blessed Saviour will set you free from that 'fear of man which bringeth a snare.'  That you will still be the subject of 'fear and trembling' while engaged in so momentous a work as that of calling sinners to repentance is not improbable; yet be sure of the reason, so that you may have the happiness of knowing you are privileged to suffer for Christ.  But do not condemn yourself without occasion.  We cannot help wishing to avoid reproach or humiliation, and when we do violence to our feelings and continue to maintain our determination to work for Christ, that is suffering in His cause, while at the same time we may be conscious of a mixture of motive which we cannot help deploring.  'If thine eye be single thy whole body shall be full of light.'

"This singleness of purpose God will grant us on our persevering importunity.  Venture upon Christ without regard to your unworthiness; and when you feel as if your prayers were doing you no good, do not let this dishearten you in the least: still *trust*.

"Sometimes Jesus calls His disciples apart to rest

awhile now, as He did in the days of His flesh, and you need not be at all surprised after the conflicts through which you have been called to pass, before and on Sunday, at this inactive frame. It is indeed necessary to your continuance in your work. If your mind were constantly on the alert your frame would soon wear out. But whatever you may feel or not feel, it is always your privilege to *trust*. If you are in doubt whether God attends to such prayers as we offer when our feelings are dull, just consider whether you do not really desire the things for which you ask; whether they are not in accordance with the will of God, and whether if you really do desire blessings of God, He will withhold them because your desire seems so languid from the effect of previous excitement. Remember you come to a kind and tender parent who is 'touched with the feeling of our infirmities.' How gracious a word is this.

"Then think again, if you had an opportunity of having an interview with the real person of Jesus, whether you would make the peculiar state of your feelings an excuse for not availing yourself of His help and blessing; or whether or not He would make the granting of your request dependent upon your feelings. He might indeed ask, '*Believest* thou that I am able to do this ?'

"At such times as these, when we feel our own unworthiness and utter weakness, it honors God to exercise a childlike faith in Him, and be assured that if we do so, ere long the spirit of prayer will return to us.

"Sometimes for days together I have had this apathy to contend with ; but as I never let it hinder me from the performance of known duty, I feel that there is no cause for discouragement, and, perhaps, for a temperament like mine, it is necessary. It is, at any rate, a trial of one's faith, and a great one; therefore, we shall not be the losers if we only *act* faith.

"I am glad you have been enabled to cast your burdens partially at least upon God. Just answer all suggestions to anxiety thus :—' My Heavenly Father tells me to cast all my care on Him, to take no anxious thought for any temporal matter, only to seek first the Kingdom of God, etc.,' and I know He will not fail to fulfil His promise that 'all these things shall be added.'

" As far as my experience and observation go, the most sure, the most blessed way to promote our temporal interests, is to put them completely into the hands of God; and I now see it is your privilege, as a preacher of the Gospel, to give yourself 'to prayer and ministry of the Word.' While you attend to God's work He will take care of your interests, and though you may be disappointed in not being able to do for others just as you would like, still I have the strongest assurance that this will turn out for the glory of God. You shall have, if you only believe, just what your Father sees best for a trusting, obedient child.

" One thing I have thought of mentioning to you, and that is, try and get your people to pray for you. Be as unreserved as is prudent, and do seek to gain their affection. This you cannot do more effectively than by asking them to pray for you, and for the success of the Word. If you could, it would be well to get a few

B

of them to meet at stated times to pray especially for these objects.

"I will just give you an extract I have met with on the benefit of suffering :—

"As grass and flowers spring up where the rain falls, so beautiful and sweet experiences spring up where tears drop. And some day reveals to us—for moral growths require time—that we are deeper, more earnest, more tenderly sensitive to a thousand influences for the sufferings we have endured. We sooner or later learn that our manhood is larger, and that the framework thereof is stronger, for the trouble we have endured. No true man ever went through a great trouble without feeling, when he came out at the other side of it, 'I am stronger.' "

"You say it would be an awful thing if you should leave the place where you are without accomplishing any good ; so it would, but let each day bear 'some good report to heaven.' Live now, and you are sure to live in the future.

"The only way to secure the satisfaction of knowing that your labor is not in vain, is to keep close to Christ by a full surrender.

"When I read what you said about 'uncontrollable palpitation,' the words of the apostle came to my mind forcibly; Hebrews xi. 34, 'Out of weakness were made strong,' etc. I understand your feeling exactly. For some months I was engaged in a work which was of such a nature that a very small circumstance would have marred the whole thing. The whole responsibility coming upon me, and Satan desiring to overthrow it, whenever we were to have a meeting for consultation with reference to its interests, I was, despite my most stren-

uous efforts, completely unable to control my feelings.
The plan I took was to get one or two faithful ones to
pray beforehand with me, and lay the cause completely
before God, that nothing might be permitted to interfere
with His will concerning it, and then I went with feelings, which you have described better than I could; and
the Lord heard prayer, baffling every effort to oppose
the work, and making His strength perfect in my
weakness.

"May you ever be enabled to realize that 'greater is He
that is for you, than all that can be against you.'

"I lately heard mentioned something concerning Luther,
which I do not recollect to have seen or heard before.   It
was his practice to take a peculiar promise suited to his
circumstances, and plead thus :—

"'Lord here is this promise and it belongs to me ; now
if Thou dost not fulfil this promise to me, I will never
believe Thee again,' etc.

"This appears at first sight to be the height of presumption, but it was doubtless the utterance of that strong
faith in the truthfulness of Jehovah which characterized
Luther.   Then, again, it was the language of intense
earnestness which shut him up to that desperate mode of
pleading.   If this manner of Luther's had been displeas-
ing to God, he would not have received such remarkable
answers to prayer, neither would he have been so highly
honored of God as to be made the means of such an in-
calculable amount of good to his fellow-men.

"I am just now beginning to prepare for my industrial
school; have taken the lower flat of a house, and intend

to get it fairly on foot before sending out circulars to inform the public. Shall go on Müller's plan entirely; that is, I shall ask no one to contribute, and no expedients will be restored to, to raise money, except such as the Bible recommends or approves.

"Ever your loving Mother,

"A. B. JOHNSON.

"P. S.—Do not fail to write anything and everything."

————

April 26th, 1867.

"MY VERY DEAR SON,

"How much pleased we were to receive your last letter, dated April ———. The time seemed very long until we should hear whether you had really undertaken the important charge which had been proffered to you.

"Doubtless you will have very many things unpleasant to contend with, many things repugnant to your sensitive mind, but recollect, Jesus requires us to take up our cross *daily* and follow Him. Think what an honor it is to be employed for the Redeemer, and what a yet greater honor to suffer for Him.

"I have just been reading the 11th of Corinthians, where St. Paul speaks of what he had passed through for the testimony of Jesus Christ, and where he appears to think these things matter of 'boasting' or 'glorying.'

"Returning homeward this morning after a walk, I met J. M. walking up and down the sidewalk. I learned for the first time that he has an ailment in one foot which often compels him to walk the floor all night long, which accompanies him to the house of God and obliges him sometimes to leave before the close of the service; that keeps a perpetual irritation and pain while he is writing or studying or trying to rest. And this affliction is of ten years' standing. He says he used to murmur at it, but now he sees it must have been one of his greatest blessings.

"Had it not been for this, he thinks he would now have been in the 'open field of ruin.' Yet it is an awful 'thorn in the flesh.' He has been advised to have his foot taken off at the ankle to prevent the disease from going up higher and endangering his life, and he is strongly inclined to submit to the sad alternative. I asked him if he had received any injury by which he could account for the ailment. He said no, the pain is in the bone, and such is the heat of the foot, to which he applies cold water, that in a few minutes after putting on a wet towel it will be steaming as if it came out of hot water.

"Oh, I thought, what would I do if this happened to one of my sons ! Can you think of anything in your circumstances approaching this in painfulness ?

"And yet this is not so bad as to be deprived of the power of moving about, as many around us are. There is a person living near us who has lost the use of her lower limbs entirely ; she said to me one day, ' When I think of the little things which once tried me, and compare them with this terrible inability to help myself, I am amazed that I could have been so stupid.'

"She is a Christian, but has never entirely risen above her affliction ; though she is resigned, yet her sorrows are great, inasmuch as she is likely to live a long time without any prospect of relief.

"You, no doubt, meet with many new and strange experiences in your new abode, but if you can do anything to save the souls of the people you must be thankful. I do wish we could help you to put on a cheerful courage ; am glad you find the effort generally successful when you try to do so.   There is a glorious future* for you, whether you see it or not ; you cannot endure or accomplish anything for Christ but what will tend to augment your treasure in the skies.

"You cannot realise how greatly we feel interested in your present circumstances ; you will be continually remembered at a throne of grace.   Do not fail to get the habit of drawing largely from God's bounty in secret.   Do not engage in anything without first waiting upon God. This *waiting on God* signifies more than just offering up our prayers ; it means that we wait in expectation of an answer.   Oh, this unbelief !   How much we should pray against it.

"The Lord help you to realise that however unworthy you may be, still all the Divine resources are at your command.

---

*These words seem almost like a prophecy in view of the fact that after six short years of ministry, the well-beloved son was suddenly called upwards ; lifted out of the scenes in which, by reason of his morbidly sensitive spirit, he was always more prone to sorrow than to joy.  The field of labor was indeed changed several times, but the tender self-accusing conscience remained.

" I am glad you feel confidence that all the difficulties which surrounded you when your letter was written, would be undertaken by your Heavenly Father. You are not ' going a warfare at your own charges.' You are working for a good and beneficent Master. Consult with *Him* as often as possible ; cast *all* your care on Him. How glad I am to know 'He careth for you.'

" I received yesterday a letter from your uncle A. D.W., dated Glasgow, 8th April. He is rather sick of the sea and is going to leave it ; is about to visit the French Exposition and then, if he can get ' an interpreter ' will visit Yorkshire and hunt up our sixteenth cousins (your grandfather was a Yorkshireman), ' and see if they profess the Buddhist religion or the Mahometan.' He sent a paragraph from a paper which runs thus :—

" 'A gentleman who went as a passenger on the good ship *Oracle* on her last trip to Honolulu, speaks in terms of the highest possible praise as to the conduct of Capt. A. D. Wood, commander of the vessel.

" ' The crew consisted of representatives of five different nations, and if knocked down, cursed, tricked, gagged, tied up, whipped and hazed generally from morning till night, might have been as bad as it is alleged were those of the great *Republic* or *White Swallow* ; but on the contrary, not an oath was heard, not a blow struck ; everything went on like clock-work, and every order of the Captain and officers was obeyed the moment given. The *Oracle* made the quickest trip out this season, namely, eleven days, two hours—and her passengers, instead of hurrying out as if to escape from a pestilence, left their comfortable quarters on a well-regulated vessel with a feeling something akin to that experienced on leaving home.'

"I am so thankful to have a letter from my brother after being so long in suspense ; and to have such testimony in his favor as that scrap of paper bore.

"Temperance is progressing favorably here. One saloon after another is being closed. M—h's sign is down, and his place is never to be rented for liquor-selling again. Is not that a special answer to prayer ?

"Your affectionate Mother.

"A. B. J."

---

" April 5th, 1867.

" MY DARLING LITTLE DAUGHTER,

"I received yesterday your interesting letter containing an account of your perplexities, and the request that I would give you some advice.

"You may think it strange, but I find this a difficult thing to do. For one reason, the subject is of great importance, and for another, your interests lie so near my heart that if I should fail to give you the right counsel, the result being loss to you instead of benefit, I should be exceedingly sorry.

"You must try to act up to your convictions, but do not suppose that you must bear about a constant burden in reference to what is your duty. You ask if the faithful discharge of your ordinary duties is not serving God Certainly it is. Doing all we have to do 'heartily as unto the Lord.' This is acceptable in His sight, and where this faithful discharge of duty is *seen* to spring from a principle of love to Christ, there is no computing the amount of good it may be the means of doing in a place where you are surrounded with those who, like yourself, are trying to serve God. I look upon it that you can be the means, by your words and actions, by the spirit you manifest, of helping-forward in the way of holiness those who are trying to walk in the fear of God; that this is of as much importance as the work of saving souls, because, if Christians are stimulated to their duty, God will make them instruments of saving souls.

"Cast all your care upon God in reference to the work you are called on to perform. Tell the Lord all your fears and perplexities, and give Him the fullest confidence, as one who sympathizes in all your feelings, and who is more ready to supply your wants than you are to ask.

"Do not be afraid for the future; if you have present help from the Lord, leave the future entirely to Him, remembering that He has said, "My grace is sufficient for you."

"It is necessary that your faith should be tried, but it is always your privilege to trust. Do not be afraid of presumption. If you do really consecrate all to God, as I believe you do, resolutely believe you are accepted, no matter how you feel. 'Reckon yourself dead to sin and alive to God.'

"You will have trials, but remember what a glorious thing it is to suffer in order to augment that 'exceeding weight of glory ' which we are to enjoy in the upper and better world.

"Go to prayer with your mind made up to believe that what you ask will be given, if in accordance with His will. He wants you to be "a burning and shining light,' and I think you are placed in favorable circumstances for this.

"But when you have asked any special blessing from God, do not think because the answer does not come just in the way you look for it, that therefore it is not granted. It may be delayed, but rest upon God without anxiety; just let Him appoint you your work.

" Hold yourself in readiness to perform your duty, and even though the way may not seem as clear to you to make an effort for Him, as you desire, and you may seem to lose an opportunity of doing your duty, expect that He will show you more clearly, and remember that He does forgive past errors. 'Like as a father pitieth His children, so the Lord pitieth them that fear Him.'

"Now, my dear, if when you read this letter you find that you do not come up to the mark, do not fret about it or be at all uneasy; you must be content to learn one lesson at a time. Having committed yourself to the guidance of the great Teacher, remember He will guide you into all truth.

" By whatever means your mind becomes enlightened in these great truths of the Gospel, it is through the mercy of God in Christ Jesus. And oh ! what wonderful things God will show you if you are determined to make a constant and full surrender of all to Him. Just think of this promise, 'If ye abide in Me, and My words abide in you, ye shall ask what ye will, and it shall be done unto you.' 'And *whatsoever* ye shall ask the Father in My name, He will give it to you.'

"See what blessings you can call down on your parents, brothers and sisters ; and we all need your prayers. Whatever you desire for these you can ask God to bestow, whether it relate to spiritual or temporal blessings. Remember when you come to God, it is upon some important errand you are coming, and attend to it with just as much belief that your wishes will be fulfilled, if they are in accordance with His will, as you have that, when you study your lessons faithfully, you will reap the advantage and be approved rather than condemned.

"If these hints will be of any value I shall be glad.

"Your loving Mother,

"A. B. J.

—————

"Nov. 30th, 1866."

"MY VERY DEAR E.,

"My first thoughts on awakening this morning were directed to Heaven in yours and T.'s behalf, that the blessing of the Lord might descend upon you ' as the dew upon the tender herb.' That showers might descend upon your souls, as they were descending upon the earth ; that your souls might be fruitful in all the graces of the Spirit, and that you might be all light in the Lord.

"I wonder if you do not, both of you, feel oftentimes on your first waking, depression and anxiety, and a fear that you will get but little assistance and little enjoyment from prayer. Never yield to these feelings for a moment; now, before these habits of mind become confirmed, resist this tendency to discouragement, no matter what your duties are, however pressing. Still hold on to the belief that God will help you, and that you will gain the victory. What if you are unworthy; God is your Father, and if even an earthly parent takes delight in forgiving a repentant child, how much more that gracious Father in Heaven, who 'counts the hairs of our head,' and has graven us upon the palms of His hands.

" How it must grieve the blessed Spirit when we feel afraid to approach unto God, or when we do so more from a sense of duty than from a certain expectation of receiving a blessing. There is nothing in which we are called upon to engage, in which we may not confidently expect the help of our gracious Friend above, if we only ask in faith.

" What does Christ mean when He says, ' Have faith in God.' That we act as if we believed what God has said. He says to you, ' Fear not, I am with thee; be not dismayed, I am thy God; I will help thee,' etc.

" Let us then wait upon God with a childlike confidence, and He will supply all our need. ·

" I would give worlds, if I possessed them, to have my two lovely boys little children about me again, with the experience I now have. But, as I cannot have this, I avail myself of the only resource left, for which I ought to be, and am, very thankful. I have been pleading with the Lord that He would place you and T. where circumstances would be favorable to the development of the best traits of character; I feel as though I could never pray enough about these things.

"'And the Lord, He it is that doth go before thee, He will be with thee, He will not fail thee neither forsake thee; fear not, neither be dismayed.'"

"Can you realize that such a passage is for you! Do try and comfort yourselves with these words. Try to feel that God is close by you always; what would become of you if He were not? If any day passes in which you do not signally fail, or in which you do not meet with some trial or humiliation, ascribe it to God alone, do not fail to give Him the glory. But remember that—

> "'Crosses in His sovereign hand
> Are blessings in disguise.'"

"Is it not strange that I can contemplate the fact of you both being away without any regret? Were it not for the privilege of praying for you, I could not do so. I know I am impelled to pray for you more frequently than if you were at home; you *seem* to be more exposed, whether you are or no, and I have more leisure to pray for you. My anxieties have always been so great for your advancement in whatever goes to make up excellence of character, that that is the all-absorbing consideration, now that you are away.

"May the Lord in His great love bless you both.

"Your loving Mother,
"A. B. J."

TO HER DAUGHTERS.

25th Nov., 1866.

My Dear A: and M.,

I so often find myself hurried when I put off
writing until the set day for it, that I have thought I
would vary my plan for once, and sit down now to give
you some portion of the history of this day. This is
Sunday. It is now half-past three o'clock, and I have
just returned from a visit to a sick young woman of
of whom Mr. L. told me last night. She has lately come
from Woodstock; has been in poor health for four years,
but has only been confined to her bed about three weeks.
She is quite resigned and prepared to die.

But I must begin with the morning. At ten o'clock I
went, as usual, to the jail; there was not one prisoner;
the matron told me the last one had been released this
morning.

Having time enough, and having provided myself with
some little books, I walked away up to the head of town
to see a poor family by the name of W. Found them just
at their breakfast. Curiosity (not idle) led me to notice
what they had on the table. Their meal consisted of
buckwheat pancakes cooked on the close stove in the
middle of the room, some kind of tea without milk, and
something on a plate that looked like butter. This is the
family of whom I wrote before, consisting of a drunken
father, a mother, and four children. It was here I had
brought the parcel of patchwork. The woman was very

glad to see me.   I asked her, " Do any of your little girls
go to Sunday-school ? "

" No ma 'am, I can 't get any clothes fit for them, but
the eldest one wants to go very much.   I've been trying
to get a little work so as to provide better for them, but
as I can 't leave my children and go out, I can get but
little to do."

" But," said I, " you have enough to do for your own
family without taking in any work."

" Yes ma 'am, I have all my wood to saw and everything to do for them " (her husband is away in the lum-
ber woods now,) " but if I could get work I would be
willing to do a good deal."

I promised to see at once about getting clothes for
them, so this will be work  for me to-morrow.

" Friday, 30th.

"To-day I received your and M's letters with the cata-
logue. I also received a short letter from T., dear child ! he
writes very affectionately. I must write him a line, though
I have just finished a long letter to E., and must write to
your Papa, who is away in St. John."

(Here follow some remarks with reference to a little
annoyance about which her daughters had written, and
she adds the following judicious advice) :—

" It is quite natural you should feel a little curious about
it, but do not let it worry you in the least; you will always be subject to such little trials, and the best way in
the world is to commit them in childlike confidence to
God.   Do not allow yourself to endeavor to find out the

reasons of such things, as you will be almost sure to come to wrong conclusions, neither allow any such mysterious conduct to lessen your regard for an individual; rather strive the more carefully to merit the approbation of such an one, or to avoid everything that would have a tendency to make you appear unamiable.

"Do not think your teachers unreasonable, and never for a moment indulge a *don't care* spirit. My dear children, you cannot be too jealous over yourselves; you cannot be too watchful of your spirits. Seek to have the lowliness and gentleness, and meekness of Christ; cultivate love towards all around you, and avoid all feelings of resentment as you would an infectious disease.

"I remain,

"Your loving Mother,

"A. B. J."

—————

"March 8th, 1867.

"MY VERY DEAR SON,

"We were much gratified with the letter received from you on Wednesday; so thankful to find you getting on so nicely.

"Do not yield to that fearfulness of disposition, but fly at once to the *Strong* for strength. Perhaps it is well to have this abiding fear of ourselves and this sense of weakness, because it ought to lead us constantly to seek that aid from above without which all our endeavours will be in vain, so far as the true object of life is concerned.

"Now, as we have no moral strength naturally, and consequently are compelled to look for it from another and higher source, we have after all, nothing to fear or to produce much uneasiness of mind.   As we need not look for anything good or wise, or strong in ourselves, however favorable our circumstances, and are obliged to be under obligation to God for every good thought, word or action, what have we to vex and disturb us ?   Is God unwilling to bestow His gifts ?   Is it for His glory that we should be ever mourning over our short-comings ?   No; let us remember that He is willing ; that He is desirous to make us monuments of His power, and mirrors to display His image.

"Well might we limit our expectations to partial attainments, to a small degree of the enjoyment of God, if it depended upon ourselves ; but when we know that we are privileged to 'ask and receive that our joy may be full,' and that He is 'able to do exceeding abundantly,' can we not cast all our care on Him ?

" You cannot be too careful in reference to having the mind pre-occupied with outside matters, instead of having it so filled with the grand subjects relating to our future well-being and the glory of God, as to absorb your whole being, and cause every secondary subject to be seen in its true light.

" At this time of your life, prejudices are strongest, and we should be on our guard as to what we receive as truth, and what we take up as worthy of being advocated and vindicated.

" Perhaps the Saviour's words to Martha might be applicable to many :  'Thou art careful and troubled about many things, but one thing is needful.'  Let us choose the

c

great and grand subjects of redemption as the theme of
our conversation more and more. Seek by a more diligent
study of the Bible and private prayer to know the mind
and will of God.

"We shall find in future years, after all our vigilance
and distrust of our own abilities, that we did not know a
*tithe* of our own weakness and insufficiency. In youth,
persons are so apt to be positive, and this seems almost inevitable from their constitution; but there is a possibility
of being humble, even in youth, and nothing is more lovely
in a young person than this grace of humility. May God
grant that both you and E. may be all that will secure the
love and respect of your associates, and the favor of the
God of Heaven. Try to help one another in all that is
lovely and of good report.

"Your loving Mother,

"A. B. J."

———

"15th March, 1867.

"MY DEAR SON,

"You do not know what amount of real satisfaction, and what thankfulness, your letter occasioned us.

"If you thought such an interposition on the part of
God was too much for you to expect, so we think as your
parents, that the Lord is indeed good beyond our expectations. And yet this is no more than has been asked of
God, though it has seemed to me that I was asking the
thing impossible; 'hoping against hope.'

"Yes, I have asked large blessings for you, and I try always to remember, in coming to ask, that

> "'God's power and grace are such
> None can ever ask too much.'

"Sometimes I almost tremble at the idea of the responsibility which the answers to these prayers will involve. Every degree of grace must be tried. If we will have much committed to us, we must submit to the inevitable condition. 'Where much is given, much will be required.' You perhaps will have much to suffer; this is not pleasant to contemplate.

"Sometimes you will be crushed to the earth, but there is need for it. I heard a remark of some one lately to the effect that 'crushed flowers yield the sweetest perfumes.'

"We must learn to 'endure hardness as good soldiers of Jesus Christ;' to 'count it all joy when we fall into divers *trials.*'

"Whatever suffering and toil you may be called to endure, you will always be comforted by the reflection, *this is for Christ.* These words of some author seem to be in keeping with this train of thought: 'There is enjoyment true and rational in life, even when it seems, at times, as if it could not be found. There is a path which no fowl knoweth, and which the vulture's eye hath not seen. *He* has found it, who has made it his daily task to relieve human misery, and who has seen the light of his own eyes reflected back from the grateful tears of those whom he has soothed or saved.

" ' *He* knows it, who, like the exiled pilgrim, careful even amid the cold and hunger of a wilderness, knows that he has remained faithful to God. St. Paul found it when he gloried in infirmities. To his lofty spirit the attitude of self-denial was a *bracing air* which invigorated his energies and redoubled the life which it seemed ready to *quench*. Useful services in the cause of God will change shadow to noon-day, and make pain and sorrow the rounds of a Jacob's ladder by which the soul will climb to heaven.'

" The Lord will bless you, I know. I am glad to find you speak of loving the people, and that you think so deeply of their spiritual good.

" I am considerably concerned about you taking such a fatiguing way of travelling ; why do you trust yourself to such untutored horseflesh ? Do you not think you are going contrary to the word, " Do thyself no harm ?" I am afraid you have had a fit of illness from that indiscreet ride.

" We have nothing doing here except in the way of temperance ; that cause is still progressing.

" We shall be very anxious to hear from you soon again. Do let us know the details of everything. Never let the fear of grieving us deter you from giving us a full account of your circumstances and mistakes, infirmities, etc.

" Your loving Mother,

"A. B. J."

" FREDERICTON, MAY, 20th, 1867.

" MY DARLING CHILDREN,

"We were delighted to receive such satisfactory letters from you on Saturday. Am so thankful the Lord is teaching both of you, and I hope these lessons will never be forgotten—these lessons taught by Him who taught as never man taught—and that henceforth, your motto may be 'onward and upward.'

" It is well to keep constantly before us the great end of our existence; there is no danger of minor matters going far astray if we only attend to the great subjects of the soul. Why should we wait any longer to avail ourselves of those great and glorious blessings which Christ has purchased as our right, and which He is so desirous we should have in possession.

"I am so glad dear M. is learning to cast her care on God, to leave everything in His hands, and to feel that she can trust at all times. Now, you know, as every habit is strengthened by exercise, we must continue to exercise faith, and even if we have more trials than we expect let us remember we are to be the gainers. Our faith must be tested, and if we are called to suffer in our Master's cause, this is a great privilege. No doubt there is very important work in store for you; you need not fear but it will be great enough, but it will be by the way of the cross. When the sons of Zebedee wished to have the honor of sitting on either side of Jesus in His kingdom, Jesus said, 'Ye know not what ye ask; are ye able to drink of the cup that I drink of?' etc. So when we

implore of Christ the honor of working for Him, we know
not to what trials and humiliations we shall be subjected,
in order that our prayer may be answered. Still, it is
right we should be ambitious of this honor, and we know
that 'if we suffer with Him we shall also reign with Him.'
We know, too, that His grace will be sufficient for us;
that He will be with us in six troubles, and in the seventh
He will not forsake us.

"Our Saviour commands us to 'let our light shine,' and
He never gives a command with which He does not give
the opportunity to comply; therefore, we need have
no anxiety as to what will be our sphere in the future,
only let us use the grace already given. 'He that is faithful in little is faithful also in much.' 'To him that hath
shall be given and he shall have abundance.' Act well
your present parts, seek to exhibit the Christian graces,
to get control over everything that would make your
Christian character appear deformed. ·Let there be a consistent uniform deportment, and especially cultivate
charity, which is the greatest of all the graces.

"We received on Saturday such a very nice letter from
T. He seems to take such a correct view of his depen-
dence upon God, and does appear to be growing in experience very fast. Oh, that he may be sustained and
directed in every future step in life.

"From E. we are expecting a letter daily. I do hope
nothing will interfere with his visit home this vacation;
still we must leave all this in the hands of the Lord.
How the time is drawing near for your coming, yet
patience will have to hold out a little longer. What a

mercy your health continues good.   The poor girl who is
not expected to live—I hope she is a real Christian and
is willing to depart and be with Christ—how many sorrows she will escape.

"I have chosen Monday for writing, as my Bible class
meets at four; so I have been writing since ten o'clock
this morning.   My time is up and I must close.

" Your loving Mother,

" A. B. JOHNSON."

————

" MY VERY DEAR SON,

"I hope when this reaches you, you will feel that
the Lord is indeed better to you than all your fears.

.        .        .        .        .        .

"O, dear son, I can see how good the Lord is to you,
and how great blessings He has in store for you.   Now,
let me remind you that every good gift comes from God,
and believe Him for His *works' sake,* if you cannot see
Him as you would like to do.

"I have just been thinking of Fletcher's words, 'Sin
gives you your first title to the *Friend* of sinners, and a
simple faith the second.   Do not, then, puzzle yourself
about contrition, faithfulness, love, joy, power over sin,
and a thousand other things, which Satan will try to persuade you you must bring to Christ.   He will receive you
gladly, with the great mountain of sin; and the smallest
grain of faith, at Christ's feet, will remove that mountain.

"'Do not puzzle yourself about joy or love ; only desire
that this Blessed Man may be your Bridegroom, and that

you may firmly believe that He is so, because He hath
given you His flesh and blood on the cross; continue be-
lieving this and trusting Him. Your business is with
Jesus, with His free, unmerited love, with His glorious
promises.

" 'Strongly expect no good from your own heart ; expect
nothing but unbelief, hardness, unfaithfulness. And
when you find them there, be not shaken nor discouraged ;
rather rejoice that you are to live by faith on the faithful heart of Christ, and cast not away your confidence,
which hath great recompense of reward.

" ' When you are dull and heavy, as will often be the
case, remember to live on Christ and claim the more by
faith. Jesus will teach you all day long. Look unto Him
and be saved, and remember He forgives seventy times
seven.

"This advice is intended for one who had not become
established in grace ; still, I think it is applicable to all
Christians.

"Annie is at home now ; and we find it very pleasant,
although her stay is so brief. Dear girl, she gives promise of being all that we could wish ; I see a marked improvement in her since she left us last fall.

" This is a confused and peculiar letter, but such as it is
I send it.

" Do not be afraid to express your belief in God's goodness.

" Your loving Mother.
"A. B. J."

" OTTAWA, March 28th, 1873.

" MY VERY DEAR SON,

" Another Friday finds us in the same place, and in fair health, trying to urge on our way to a better state, a happier clime.

" A blessed immortality is worth taking some trouble for. I am persuaded that a great good of any kind is not to be obtained without the sacrifice of much personal comfort, and why should we complain if the way through this wilderness is sometimes so difficult, since we have the assurance that Jesus is our Captain, and has trod the way before us, knows every hardship and danger with which we shall have to meet.

" Life seems to me more precious than ever, affording, as it does, an opportunity for the perfecting of the Christian character. For a few days past I have been almost overwhelmed at the view of the responsibilities of a human being, and astonished at the fact that we do not more fully realize the necessity of a more constant application to the source of all strength and wisdom, seeing that without help from a source foreign to ourselves, one can do nothing well.

" I hope you will never make the mistakes I have made, many of which I should have avoided had my walk been closer with God. You can never estimate the value of a habit of private prayer. This the enemy will strive above all things to thwart you in, for he knows it is a bad sign of a Christian when he does not enjoy private prayer better than any other. Until we get the victory over this enemy to our souls, so that we shall find it a happy exercise to pour out our souls in private prayer, we shall never have power with God or man.

"Now here is an object worthy of attention. This power we can have, and in no other way than by waiting on God in private. Only let us persevere. We must be emptied of all self before God can take up His abode in us.

"Let us not yield for a moment to the suggestions that our prayers are not being answered. According to our faith it shall be done to us, and faith waits and listens for His voice. Wait on the Lord by looking into His word and meditating on His character and the great things He has done for us.

"Your Loving Mother,

"A. B. J."

———

To her daughter M., who was away on a visit:—

"OTTAWA, April 21st, 1875.

"MY DEAR CHILD,

"I think I told you about H. J. calling to tell me he had signed the pledge. Poor soul, he was trembling with weakness and nervousness the next day, when he called to get a pair of boots I had promised him; but he had washed himself, and in spite of his rags he looked more hopeful. Indeed, I began to feel more faith for him. He had remained all night with a friend, had risen very late and taken breakfast about eleven, and said that, though he was terribly shaken, he still felt better for sound sleep, that he had made up his mind *never*, *never* to taste another drop.

"When I told him that if he would call again before he went away, I would give him some clothes, ' I don't deserve them,' said he.

" ' I know you do not,' said I ' but the weather is cold, and you would suffer without them.'

" ' I am very thankful to you,' said he.

" Late in the afternoon he came again, looking so *woebegone* that I was willing to take any trouble for the poor victim. (Of course I had before talked kindly to him and given him all the encouragement in the world.) So I went and got him a complete suit of clothes, including a hat.

" ' Now,' said I, ' you can go to church to-morrow, and to the temperance meeting.'

" ' Yes,' said he, ' that is why I came up this afternoon. I wanted to go to them places and had nothing to wear, but these will look *well*. I shall never forget your kindness.'

" I begged him to call upon God for help, and not to depend upon his own exertions.

" He said, ' Oh, I have been praying, indeed I have.'

" Do you know I have strong faith for the poor man. I have seldom realized so much satisfaction in doing an act like that of supplying him with clothes. You know how often I have given these things when I was afraid I was only helping on the rumsellers."

"FREDERICTON, Jau. 16th, 1863.
"MY DEAR FRIEND,

"I feel very grateful for the warm reception my
poor effusions have met at your hands, though I am
sure you have very much overrated them. But, as it
is not natural to be exceedingly annoyed with commendation, when it happens to be bestowed on ourselves or on
our own productions, I do not feel in the humor for scold-
ing you, or even of trying to prove you deficient in judgment. The most I will venture to say is, he must be a
wonderful man who *never* allows his prejudices to influence his opinions.

"Seriously, my dear friend, if you knew what a coward
I am, and how very much dissatisfied I have always been
with my own performances (in the writing line as well
as every other), you would not wonder at my being gratified, and thankful for such a cheering answer to my scribbling, as your dear, kind letter furnished. I do assure
you that such is my sense of my utter insufficiency to do
anything as *I should like to do it*, that, were it not for
the constraining influence of the Gospel on my heart, and
a degree of crucifixion of nature, which enables me to exercise a willingness to be anything or nothing in the eyes
of others, so that God may be glorified, I should never
commit myself by putting forth an effort that would expose me to criticism.

"This constitutional timidity has often hindered me,
or I have allowed it to hinder me doing many things
which I might have done for God, and consequently I

have suffered loss, inasmuch as, if I had improved my talent better, I should now have been better fitted for usefulness.

" I have, however, come to this point ; when I am persuaded of my duty, I dare not yield to any suggestion of unfitness, because Christ says ' My grace is sufficient for thee.' 1 feel sure that it is ' not by might, nor by power, but by My Spirit, saith the Lord.' The feeblest instrument may be rendered powerful through the Divine blessing. This conviction enables me to pursue a course of self-denial, to bear crosses which I should once have thought it impossible to carry. To be willing, if need be, to be reproached ; to have my judgment called in question (this is very hard to nature), and to rejoice when I was made partaker of Christ's sufferings. My dear friend, if you knew what grace has done for *me*, you would feel there is amazing power in it, and it would encourage you to go and proclaim its riches and glories to your fellow mortals, which may God grant to inspire you with a quenchless zeal to do !

" You say, ' I am deeply indebted to you, etc, and the worst of it is I cannot recompense you.' Oh, my dear friend, if you have derived any benefit whatever from anything I have said, is not that a sufficient reward for the feeble service I have rendered you ? Am I not more than repaid already in the hope that having ' stirred up your pure mind by way of remembrance ' you may be induced to ' give more earnest heed ' to those things which relate to our peace. I feel urged to persuade you to an acceptance of all the glorious things of the children of

God.   Why should you be 'insignificant' in the world
of glory ?   Why should you not have an abundant entrance there ?   Why should you not hear, 'Well done,
good and faithful servant.'   There is nothing in your circumstances to prevent it.   There is nothing in the plan
of the Almighty to prevent it.   Your past deplored unfaithfulness will not prevent it.

" It was not the repeated acts of rebellion and the long
course of unfaithfulness of which the children of Israel
had been guilty, that prevented their entering into the
promised land.   They had every assurance that not-
withstanding all this that glorious possession was acces-
sible to them, and nothing but their refusing the proffered gift, when they might have accepted. it on complying
with God's conditions, excluded them from the bounteous
inheritance which God had provided for them.   Think
what an amount of treasure you may yet accumulate for
heaven.   Just reflect what may be done for Christ in the
course of one, two, three or ten years.   See how much
time there is before us, if God spare.

" I remember reading in Boardman's ' Higher Life ' an
account of a man who had became a Christian, and had
led a very consistent life for forty years.   He then at the
age of sixty, was enabled to consecrate himself ' a living
sacrifice' to God, and although he lived but two years
afterwards, it was stated that he was made the means of
the conversion of multitudes, and was heard to say of
himself, that he had done by the grace of God, since
his consecration, vastly more for God in the last two years
of his life than he had done for forty years of partial con-

secration to His service. His death was not only happy but triumphant."

Your sincere friend,

A. B. J.

One by one the sands are flowing,
  One by one the moments fall ;
Some are coming, some are going,—
  Do not strive to grasp them all.

One by one thy duties wait thee,
  Let thy whole strength go to each ;
Let no future dreams elate thee,
  Learn thou first what these can teach.

One by one bright gifts from Heaven,
  Joys are sent thee here below ;
Take them readily when given,
  Ready, too, to let them go.

Every hour that fleets so slowly
  Has its task to do, or bear ;
Luminous the crown, and holy,
  If thou set each gem with care.

                              A. A. Proctor.

## III.

The letters which follow were written by the daughter to whom allusion has already been made, chiefly to her younger sisters, though shared by all the family.

This correspondence with her home circle was a source of great delight to Annie herself, and doubly so to those who received the semi-weekly letters. While aware that no smallest incident of her life could be uninteresting to her parents, brothers and sisters, and while detailing such with fidelity, she also aimed at the improvement of the latter, and could not bear that any opportunities enjoyed by her, should be unshared by them.

The reader can hardly fail to observe in her letters evidences of an ardent and enthusiastic temperament, united with diligence in study, strong affection for family and home, and the power of communicating to others that which she acquired.

Of the short, fatal illness which brought this promising career to a sudden termination, four days after her twenty-first birthday, on Sept. 11th, 1869, a more detailed account is given at the close of the letters.

"In small proportions we just beauty see ;
And in short measures life may perfect be."

D

### 1867-1868.

"February 15th.

" DEAR MAMMA,   .

"Friday, our writing day, brings another dear
letter from you. I cannot tell what a delight your
letters are to us ; but what will it be when we see each
othe r once more !Can I have the courage to leave home
again, for another long year at school ?   Of course I can ;
but it seems incomprehensible now.

"How swiftly this year is going ; I only fear you will
not see that improvement in us which you have a right
to expect; but we'll not anticipate.

"We are deeply interested in Gail Hamilton's ' New
Atmosphere.'   T. wrote to us to get it at once, without
fail, and read it.   I do wish you would get it, mamma.
I am not quite sure that you would fully endorse her sentiments ; but I'd like very much to know what you would
think of the book.   It is written to show what women's
true sphere is.   There is such energy and life in the book.
She inveighs loudly against the pernicious practice of
bringing up girls to consider marriage the chief end of
life.   There are some cutting remarks about the miserable
wages which women receive for their work, and she
quotes the following article from a Massachusetts paper :
—' The custom of employing ladies as clerks in the public departments at Washington is meeting with increased
favor.   It is said that, generally speaking, they write
more correctly than the men ; and as they receive much

smaller salaries the gain to the government is considerable.'

" Oh! how she talks about it! You would at least
admire her sentiments in regard to women spending so
much time in housekeeping, especially in cooking; and
also about dress. Her views seem just about right to
me.

" Gail Hamilton's real name is Abigail Dodge; she
resides near Boston, and graduated at Ipswich, the school
hallowed by memories of Mary Lyon. She is said to be
a very eccentric woman.

" What do you think about women voting? I suppose
you know that the question has come up before the Senate.
I heard that they were debating about allowing the
Negroes of some State to vote, and one of the Senators
said in derision, ' What! would you let the Negroes vote
and not the angels!'

" Don't you think it might tend to increase the general
intelligence of women? I'm sure I don't know what to
think about it, but I wish I did.

" I wish Papa would enlighten us in reference to
politics in the Provinces and elsewhere. We get but
little time for reading, especially now, as we have been
advanced in Latin.

" Mr. Durant came to the Seminary to-day. He is a
great friend of the Institution, and a most devoted Christian. He is very handsome in appearance and withal
very talented, a lawyer by profession. He is to lead the
meeting this evening and I must retain some room for his
address, or a sketch of it.

"Saturday Morning.

"The address from Mr. Durant was solemn and eloquent.   He will probably remain here for some days, and we will often have the privilege of listening to him.

"But I must stop now, dear mamma; please give much love to everybody.

"From your affectionate Daughter,

"ANNIE G. JOHNSON."

————

"Feb. 17th, 1867.

"DEAR MAMMA,

"We had a meeting in the Seminary Hall last night, and Mr. Durant spoke to the Christians about working for Christ.   I wish you could have heard it; it was beautiful, but mostly on account of his great earnestness, and his great, loving heart which shone out in every sentence. He first related an incident which occurred in Providence, Rhode Island, within a few weeks, I think, in connection with the Young Men's Christian Association.   Some of these young men were praying earnestly, and had been doing so for a long time, for the thousands of young men in that wicked city who were being led to destruction. One night, about six of them went to a gay saloon where crowds of people were collected, engaged in drinking and gambling.   They saw a piano on a platform in the room, and asked the proprietor if they might sing, he consented readily, and, to the astonishment of the company, they sang, ' Rock of Ages, cleft for me.'   They then asked if they might hold a prayer meeting right there, but the proprietor said he was afraid *selling rum and praying* would not go very well together, but if they wished they could come the next evening, and he would not sell any liquor. Before they went away, they persuaded about forty young men to go with them to the Christian Association.

"According to engagement, they went back the next evening, and found a large company awaiting them. As the meeting went on, others would come in, and, after gazing around in astonishment at the strange scene, would go up to the proprietor and ask what it meant, when he would explain that they were having a prayer meeting. They prayed most earnestly that the saloon might be closed up, or dedicated to holier purposes, and that the proprietor might be converted—all in his hearing. Now, Mr. Durant says, he attends prayer meetings regularly, and they have firm faith that he will be converted.

" He related several other incidents where the labors of those lately converted had been greatly blessed, showing that, though a young lady's work might be different, her sphere of usefulness was quite as extensive as that of a young man. His earnest appeals to the unconverted seem irresistible. This afternoon he spoke of the love of God, taking for his text, 'God so loved the world that He gave His only begotten Son, that whosoever believeth on Him should not perish, but have everlasting life.' This was addressed particularly to those who said they had no feeling on the subject of religion. His appeal to unconverted fathers and mothers was almost dreadful in its solemnity

" February 22nd, 1867.

"DEAR PAPA,

"I read in one of the papers here that Prince
Albert is to be our first Governor-General, when the confederation arrangements are completed; is it so? And
again I hear that we are not to have confederation after
all, that England does not wish it; and is it true that the
*wisest* men in Nova Scotia are opposed to it? I wish I
knew something about anything!

"We are still studying, eating, and sleeping, day after
day, with but little variation. Our studies are progressing finely.

"Our reading class is almost a course of gymnastics;
we had quite an amusing time to-day. Miss Ward is our
teacher, and she told us all to rise and stand in a line,
when each one was to draw in a long breath so as to fill
the lungs, and castigate the shoulders of her next neigh-
bour with a rapid percussion movement of the hands;
the alacrity with which we obeyed, and the unwonted
energy displayed were quite striking, and doubtless satisfactory to Miss Ward. We then had to 'right about
face,' and an opportunity was given us to reciprocate,
which, to judge by the clatter that ensued, did not pass
unimproved. Miss Hazen requested us all to read something in the papers to tell in sections every Thursday.
I think it a good plan, but it seems as if I had to read
almost every paper before I could get anything suitable.
My item to-day was about the threatened rebellion in

India; it is quite serious, is it not? I know nothing of the cause.

"Miss Hazen told us that the trial of Surratt is soon to commence; it will probably be deeply interesting. I hear that there is great suffering in Newfoundland, etc.

---

### TO HER LITTLE SISTER.

"April 4th, 1867.

"DARLING A.,

"Vacation is a very funny kind of time, but it is quite pleasant. Last evening we all got into a dull, listless state, and so we resolutely jumped up and had a regular dashing game of 'blind man's buff.'

"Just think of it A.; eight tall young ladies flying about the room in such style; but it had the desired effect, and I'm sure we all slept better for it. I asked Mrs. L. this morning if she had heard any unusual noise, and she said 'yes indeed,' but she did not mind how much noise we made as long as we did not come through the floor, for we were *frightening away all the rats in the house.* Imagine our pleasure at hearing of such beneficial results from our folly!

---

"February 28th, 1867.

"DEAR MAMMA,

"We have had the privilege to-day of seeing two missionaries, and the Secretary of the American Board.

" Miss Norcross graduated from this school last year, and she is just going out to India as a missionary ; Miss Warfield goes also, to Turkey, as a teacher in the Harpoot Seminary.

" It has been very interesting to see these ladies. Miss Warfield was here only a few hours, but they all went away together this afternoon. A company of six left the Seminary all together, and every teacher was outside witnessing the departure. Mrs. Stoddard looked up and saw two heads in every window in front of the building, and she signified to them that she wanted them to sing, ' Ye Christian Heralds, go proclaim.'

" After this they sang the Missionary hymn ; it was a thrilling sight, mamma, so appropriate. I never felt any-thing of the interest in missionary labor before, that I do now ; we hear so much about the work, and these foreign schools seemed intimately connected with our Seminary, from the fact that graduates from here always have charge of them, or almost always.

" In Turkey they have Theological schools for young men, in which the Bible is the only study; not because they think other studies are unnecessary, but the young men are not prepared for more yet, and with the thorough knowledge of the scriptures which they obtain, they be-come very useful as preachers and teachers.

" In Harpoot Seminary, which is on the same plan as this, there are forty girls, many of them Christians, and all anxious to learn. There is another Seminary at Oroomiah, but I don't know so much about that.

"Dr. Clark, the secretary of the American Board, gave us some very interesting accounts of the Mission work; he seems to be a [very good and talented man. I forgot to tell you of another young lady who is also going to Turkey; she is Miss Seymour, and I must try and tell how Dr. Clark procured her for the service. He had gone to a certain town to see a young lady whom he thought might be willing to go. (They were exceedingly anxious to get a teacher, as there was danger of the school going down.) At tea time he commenced talking to this young lady, to see what her sentiments might be, taking this Seminary and the great need of more laborers, as his theme; he was soon disappointed to find that her health would not permit her to go, though she was much interested in this subject; he continued talking about these things for some time, till another lady near him suddenly turned and said, 'You're not thinking of me, are you?' He had never seen her before, and told her so, adding, 'Yes, I'm thinking of you, if you're willing to go, and have a heart for the great work.'

"They had a little more conversation and then they parted, Dr. Clark having no idea that she would be persuaded to go, and in great perplexity of mind about the school.

"The next evening he attended a meeting in the same place, and after meeting, the minister said to him, 'Now you want people for your work whom we cannot spare; there is one lady here to-night who is the most useful person in this place. I cannot spare her, but if you can get her, you may have her.' He then pointed her out, and to his surprise, Dr. Clark saw that she was the same young lady he had seen the evening before. He only had time to say a few words to her before he went away. After he had reached his home, a letter came to him saying, 'Miss Seymour is thinking of going;' soon after another came from another source, to the same effect, and in a day or two more, another saying, 'Miss Seymour is going.' And so all his anxiety was relieved in this most unexpected manner. He related it as a wonderful instance of direct answer to prayer.

\*　　\*　　\*　　\*　　\*　　\*　　\*　　\*

"There was an article in the last *Independent* which rather surprised me. The subject was 'Amusement.' The writer expatiated for some time on the natural desire for amusement which every one possesses, and the necessity for that desire being satisfied in an innocent and harmless manner. Then he says that in every city there should be a house under the care of the Young Men's Christian Association, furnished with a gymnasium, *billiard tables, bowling alley*, chess, backgammon, dominoes, and many other games; with pianoes for the musical, and a room for meetings and lectures. According to this writer, the only harm connected with these games is in the associations almost invariably attending them. This establishment would be for the poorer classes and the entertainment free of charge.

"I must go to work at my composition now. So goodnight.

"Your loving Daughter,
"Annie G. Johnson."

"April 31st, 1867.

" Dear Mamma,

" So you are getting up another Ragged School.
I do hope you will succeed, as of course you will.
Perhaps a few suggestions from Mrs. Stowe's 'Sunny
Memories of Foreign Lands' may be some assistance
to you. She writes about the charitable Schools in
Aberdeen, Scotland, which had been in operation since
1841. Some benevolent persons first hired rooms, and a
teacher, and then gave out notice to the poor children
that they could there be supplied with food, work and instruction. The general arrangements were four hours of
lessons, five of work, and three substantial meals. No
child was allowed to partake of the meals who had not
been present at the work or lessons preceding them. In
this way the attendance proved to be more regular than
at ordinary schools.

" The whole produce of the children's work goes towards defraying the expenses of the establishment, thus
inculcating a spirit of independence.

" They did not profess to clothe the children, but as
they often had old clothing sent in, they were enabled to
help the more destitute ones. The scholars assemble at
seven in the summer, eight in the winter. The school is
opened by reading the Scriptures, singing and prayer.
They have lessons in Geography, and the more ordinary
facts of Natural History, from maps hung around the
walls.

" At nine they breakfast on porridge and milk, and
have half an hour of play. At ten, they again assemble

and work till two, when they dine, usually on broth and coarse bread. From dinner till three the time is spent in exercise or recreation, occasionally working in the garden ; from three to four, they work in the garden or work room; from four till seven they are instructed in reading, writing and arithmetic. At seven they have supper of porridge and milk, and after short religious exercises are dismissed to their homes. They assemble also on Sunday, but return home after dinner to go to church with their parents, returning at five, and then home again after supper.

"Separate schools were established for boys and girls, but both on the same principle.

" 'As to commencing schools in new places, the best way of proceeding is for a few persons who are of one mind on the subject, to unite, advance from their own purses, or raise among their friends, the small sum necessary at the commencement, get their teacher and collect a few scholars ; gradually extend the number, and when they have made some progress, then tell the public what they have been doing, ask them to come and see, and if they approve, to give their money and support.

" ' Let them be careful as to the parties whom they admit to *act* along with them ; for unless *all* the laborers are of one mind and heart, division must ensue, and the work be marred,'

" These are some few of the directions Mrs. Stowe quotes from an experienced teacher, and I thought they might possibly be of some use to you, and could at least do no harm. The account of the schools given in the book is

very long, and of course I could give but a very slight
synopsis of it. But do you not think one would cost
less to *you* at least got up in that way, and partly
self supporting ?

" Mrs. Stowe adds: ' there is nothing in it which may
not be easily copied in any town or village of our land
where it is required.' So much for Ragged Schools.

" On Sunday afternoon we had an address from Mr.
Woodworth, who is connected with some Society for re-
lieving the Freedmen, and it was on their behalf that he
addressed us. He was Chaplain in some company during
the war. He related some facts showing that the colored
people in the South are practically almost as much slaves
as ever.

"A man who gets seventeen dollars a month, must now
pay fifteen dollars a month for the cabin he formerly
occupied for nothing ; and multitudes of those too aged,
too young, or too infirm to work, are perishing with
hunger.

" Speaking of their intense desire for knowledge, he
illustrated it by a case of two old men he saw in a night
school. When they went to the school they did not even
know their letters, and then, after having attended for
forty evenings they could read quite fluently.

———

" May 25th 1867.

"Dear A.,

" I have only time to write a line or two, just
to give you one or two items of intelligence.

" We celebrated the Queen's birthday last night, and saw
four rattlesnakes and two copperheads ! Not that the two

circumstances were connected in any way, or consequent upon each other, but it is a fact that they both took place last evening.

" Our celebration was in the South music room, where we had music and refreshments, and ended up with ' Rule Britannia ' and ' God save the Queen.' There were just five of us ; M. F. from Canada, S. N. from Nova Scotia, and Miss N. and *we two* from N. B.

"The rattlesnakes and copperheads were brought to the Seminary for us to see, by a man who caught them a day or two ago on Mt. Tom. One rattlesnake was eighteen years old, as they judged by his rattle, and large enough to swallow a rabbit whole. Now, as I expect to go upon the mountain soon, would you not like me to catch a few and take them home with me. Good morning.

"ANNIE."

———

The first year of school had passed over ; the summer vacation been happily spent at home in Fredericton, N.B., and Annie had returned to South Hadley. In the meantime the family removed to Ottawa, Ontario, where her father subsequently became Commissioner of Her Majesty's Customs.

Her letters thereafter were addressed to Ottawa, and most of them were written to her sisters, one of whom had spent one year with her at the Seminary ; the other was the baby of the family and an especial pet with her eldest sister, who took the greatest interest in the progress of her studies, and continually endeavored to assist her by stimulating her ambition to acquire knowledge.

" Sept. 30th, 1867.

" DEAREST M.,

" The hour bell before recess meeting has just rung, and I have some little time to spend with you before I go off to room B., where our meeting is held.

" You will be interested in hearing that Miss Mary Hollister is about to go out as a missionary ; she has been in the Seminary for two or three days, but went away this morning. She addressed us for a few minutes in the Sunday evening meeting.

" This morning at breakfast Miss Ward mentioned that it had been our custom to give presents to those going out as missionaries, and any who wished could leave articles for Miss H. in the South Wing Parlor, or in Miss H's room ; she mentioned a great many small articles which would be very acceptable, and seemed anxious that we should all contribute. I came up to my room to see what could be spared from my household goods. What will mamma say when she hears that the first thing I decided upon was that lovely box of assorted tape—her useful and valued gift. Then I selected a little writing paper from each kind, and added a little box of pens, and a lead pencil, and last of all a handkerchief.

" Miss H. was surprised and delighted with the offerings of the girls ; there were all kinds of things given her, many perhaps did not give more than a spool of thread' but it amounted to a good deal in the aggregate.

" It seems to me that the ' American board ' must spend most of its time in conventions; Miss Locke has just re-turned from Buffalo, where she has been attending the meetings of the ' Board,' and gave us a very interesting account of them last night."

———

"Sept. 29th, 1887.

" In reading Shakespeare, M., the better plan will be for you to find those acts founded on some incident in Grecian history, or any history with which you are familiar. You will find it much more interesting and intelligible. If there is any act which you want to read, you can first look up the history connected with it, and so make Shakespeare a useful companion.

"The retiring bell has rung, so goodnight, my darling."

———

"Oct. 18th, 1867.

" DEAREST M.

" What will you think when I tell you that I've heard G. J. Holland (Timothy Titcomb) lecture. I enjoyed that unexpected pleasure last evening. Now, you'll want to know just how he looked, how he lectured, what about, and how I liked him. Well, he is not extraordinary in appearance, a pleasant face, but not striking; black hair and small moustache, with no whiskers. His voice is pleasant, and he speaks very distinctly. He lectured on ' Woman suffrage.' His ideas conflict completely with Gail Hamilton's; he thinks no woman is in her proper sphere outside of home and its duties, and that she ought not to vote. His lecture was very much like his writings ; in fact it would not be like itself if it was not, for he read it, much to my regret. Perhaps it was because my supper had been accompanied with a glowing eulogium on his power over an audience, his complete mastery ot language, and other perfections, that I experienced a feeling of disappointment, as the lecture progressed; but it may have been that his subject was not a very interesting one. Don't imagine, though, that he is not a very fine lecturer; I suspect that if I had not been told just before hearing him, that he was one of the finest American speakers, I would have been delighted with him.

The Amherst students were invited over to the lecture, and about twenty of the seniors came.

Mary and I have just finished reading Dr. Holland's poem, 'Kathrina.' I wish you and mamma would read it; don't like to trust my opinion, so will not give any. The '*New York Times*' has a most severe critisism on it, and that is the only comment I have seen on the work. Have you ever read 'Bitter Sweet,' by the same author? Miss Locke is reading 'Kathrina' to us in sections; she seems to admire it."

Nov. 5th, 1867.

"We have had quite a season of dissipation here; *out four evenings in one week.* The 'School Institute' for this county has held its annual session in South Hadley, and quite broken in upon the regular routine of our life. Four of its learned members stayed at the Seminary. Mr. Russel, of elocution memory; Mr. Niles, of Cambridge; Prof. Holt, a musician, and the Rev. Mr. Gage.

E

It was Mr. Russel's system of elocution that was taught at Kent's Hill, and that is generally adopted in the States. He is such a singular looking man. Tall and thin, with white hair and whiskers and always wearing a black handkerchief, in the form of a night-cap on his head; he'd look better with a *white* one, I should think. The session lasted from Monday morning till Friday night. They had seven *exercises*, or lectures every day. For instance, at 9 o'clock Mr. Russel would have an exercise in elocution. (All exercises were intended for instruction in the manner of teaching, for those who were expected to be teachers. They were conducted just as if the audience was the class, and we were questioned, and required to answer in the same way.)

" At ten Mr. Bowler, a member of Payson, Dunton and Scribner's *copy book*, would have an exercise in writing; at eleven, Miss Mitchell one on physiology, which would end the morning. At two in the afternoon, Mr. Russel would have another exercise, then some one another on arithmetic, and so on. In the evening we always had a lecture; I only heard three of them. Prof. Holt almost always finished up the evening with one of his simple, but beautiful songs. It was so interesting on Friday evening. Mr. White lectured on 'School Government.' When he stopped it was nearly ten, but he asked the audience if they would not like to wait and hear a song from Prof. Holt; of course we all would; so he brightened us up with a little comic song. We thought we were surely going then, but he reminded us that it was the custom for Mr. Russel to give a declamation before closing the evening, and there was a not very hearty call for Mr. Russel. He made his way to the platform, remarking, 'People cannot always be short and *sweet*, but I can at least be *short*.' He then recited an amusing, but instructive, piece which quite paid us for waiting; he does declaim beautifully. They then found that it would not do at all to wind up without music, so Prof. Holt was called on for 'Over the River they Beckon to me,' and last of all we all united in singing a hymn, and then dispersed.

" While the meetings continued we had half hour recitations, had no singing, gymnastics, or hall; no 'time on lessons,' and sections at the fifteen bell before supper ; just think what a change it must have made.

" Do you know Charles Dickens is to read in Boston this vacation ! What if I should hear him !

" Mr. and Mrs. Wheeler, missionaries from Kharpoot, were here for several days. Mrs. Wheeler is lovely, just suits my idea of a missionary; and Mr. Wheeler gave us some very interesting accounts of the work in Turkey. He told us that they make the native churches support themselves, as soon as there is any possibility of their doing it; holding up as an imperative duty, as well as a privilege, the giving of a tenth of everything they possess. He gave us some interesting illustrations of the great pleasure they find in doing this, and the spiritual good resulting from it.

"Nov. 7.

"DEAR M.,

"I suppose it is only a day or two since I wrote to you, but it seems pretty long, and I must write just a few lines to-night.

"Yesterday, with some other visitors, came a converted Burmese youth to visit the Seminary. He addressed us this morning after devotions, and I think has gone now. He has been in this country for ten years, fitting himself for a missionary to his own countrymen, by a study of medicine and theology; and he is just about to return to his native land. He is small in stature, looks to be about twenty years of age, has long, jet-black hair, delicate features, and very small hands. When he came into the hall to speak to us this morning, he wore a large red and yellow turban, and an immense silk scarf fastened around his vest, and flowing down to the floor, the other end thrown gracefully over his shoulder. A white necktie beside his brown complexion made him look somewhat clerical. He told us a great deal about the manners and customs of the Burmese. His manner was very easy and graceful, and he spoke our language with wonderful facility. He took off his turban and put it on again, to show us how it was done, and explained the various uses to which the silk scarf is put; it is five yards long and three breadths in width. · He was quite humorous at times. In describing their god (I forget his name), he said, 'He was said to be thirty-five feet high; his ears hung on his shoulders; his fingers reached to his knees, and he could touch his nose with his tongue, all of which were considered evidences of a divine character.' Afterwards, ' When we eat there are two waiters placed before us, one containing rice and the other various kinds of spices; we do not use spoons or knives, but a five-pronged fork like this,' holding up his hand and spreading out his fingers, carelessly adding, ' which we scour well before using.' He spoke with great affection of Dr. Judson, who lived just opposite his grandfather's house, though he could not have been more than a child when Dr. Judson was living."

---

"Jan. 16th, 1868,"

" Loved Ones At Home.

" I have not time to write to each of you individually, and being unable to decide upon the one to whom I could address my remarks, have concluded to write to all at once.

" After papa left me on Tuesday morning, I remained in the same car till it reached Rouse's Point, where I exchanged my comfortable accommodations for others very inferior, being squeezed into a seat with a strong-minded old lady, who beguiled the time with most comforting remarks about the unsafe nature of the bridge on which we were crossing Lake Champlain. We reached St. Albans early in the morning, and, mindful of the earnest injunctions I had received at Ogdensburg, jumped out to get my trunk rechecked, though I had not to change cars. I found the baggage car, and saw my trunk entirely out of my reach and being speedily overwhelmed with a mass of fresh baggage. After gazing helplessly at it for some time, and seeing no hope of accomplishing anything, I suddenly thought of the conductor, whose obliging disposition I had proved while going over the route before. On hearing my tale of distress, he readily came to my relief, and succeeded, after much difficulty, in getting the trunk checked to Northampton; meanwhile giving vent to his intense indignation at the *being who did'nt* check it as far as my ticket took me.

" By this time the position of the various trains in the station had undergone a puzzling revolution, even the conductor was unable for some time, to find his own train, and discovered it so late that I had to spring on board after it was in motion.

" The last change of cars was at White River Junction, some time in the night. In the car which I then entered, there sat a man who had stolen a horse in New York, and a detective who was escorting him back thither. The two seemed to be on the most friendly terms, which made me think that the horse stealer must have possessed a most forgiving disposition.

" Towards morning I asked the conductor if the train went on to Smith's Ferry; he said it did, but would not stop there. I wondered where I would be carried to, and how I would get back, but waited to see what the next conductor would say. On enquiring of the next one, he said I would have to change cars at Northampton, but came in shortly after and said that I might go right on, and they would stop for me; then taking my check, he attended to my trunk and gave me another check. We reached Smith's Ferry at six o'clock in the morning, of course it was quite dark. I jumped out at the station, my trunk was thrown out and the train dashed on, leaving me, a lonely wayfarer, standing in the dark and cold with the snow drifting in my face, and vainly striving to answer the question, 'What am I to do next?'

"Going up to the station house door, I cautiously pushed it open, but saw only darkness, though a sense of warmth led me to conclude that there was a fire there. Rather than venture to explore the dark recesses of the room, I preferred to walk about in the snow, and fancying that I heard voices at some distance, attempted to wade through the snow on the railway track in the direction whence came the sounds, but had to give up the attempt very soon. After pacing the creaking platform for some time longer, I became convinced that this was great foolishness, and resolved that if I could not be comfortable, I would at least be as comfortable as was possible under the circumstances; so I boldly walked into the station and proceeded to examine it as thoroughly as the very imperfect light would permit.

"After satisfying myself that I was the only occupant of the room. I drew a chair up to the stove, extracted a couple of apples from my satchel, and proceeded to their discussion.

"Meantime the dawn was slowly creeping on. By the way, if any of you are particularly desirous of cultivating your imaginations, I would advise you to place yourselves in similar circumstances. I found that without any effort on my part, any sedate and leafless shrub could be magnified into the rapidly approaching figure of a man; if the snow dashed against the window-pane, instantly there fell on my ear the music of merrily ringing sleigh bells; and indeed if sights and sounds had been of such unstable character, Smith's Ferry would have been a lively place, and I could not long have suffered for want of company.

"But there came an end to all this; for about seven o'clock a *real* man made his appearance, but for fear I might be deceived, and he too should vanish into air, I ran out and accosted him before he had reached the station. He very consolingly informed me that the stage would be there at half-past eight, so, taking up an ancient newspaper, I sat down, and tried to be resigned. Well, half past eight did arrive at last, and with it the stage. A comfortable drive of about half an hour brought me to the Seminary, and soon my feet were once more treading its corridors.

"I went right down to my room, and saw 'excused from table' on the door; on my opening it, M. looked up enquiringly, as if to say, Have you brought my breakfast?' But the truth soon dawned upon her, and depend upon it there was a scene! Poor M. had been in bed since last Friday, and was still so indisposed that Miss B. said she must go to a warmer room, accordingly M. has since been oscillating between 144 in the South Wing, and 78 which I occupy with M. T., a very nice kind-hearted girl, and I find the temporary arrangement very pleasant.

"You may imagine that the unpacking of my trunk was rather an interesting circumstance. The cake was pronounced 'splendid,' and evidence that this was no empty compliment, may be seen in the fact that there is quite an alarming gap in one of them. As I was tired out from travelling and want of sleep, I did not of course get up to our half past six breakfast this morning, the consequence of which was no less than *three very delightful* interviews with Miss W., who finally concluded that I "might be excused under the circumstances'!!

Every one seems astonished to see me. They had an impression that I was not coming back till the summer term. To my surprise I find that the new series does not commence till next week, but if I had waited it would have been no easier to come away, and it is rather an advantage to be here in such good time. Good night.

" Yours most lovingly,

" ANNIE G. JOHNSON."

"January 21st, 1868.

" We have had a visitor here for some days past. Mr. Pardee, a 'Sunday-school man,' has been talking to us on the subject of teaching in Sunday-schools. The children of a Sunday-school in Montreal presented him with a splendid suit of fur. Yesterday, our recitations were omitted that we might improve his visit the more. We had three sessions of an hour each, during the day, and in the evening Mr. Pardee went away.

"His suggestions were most valuable, and I do wish I could make them available in some way. It seems such a time before I'll be able to put them into practice myself. I took notes all the time, and have procured a blank book which I intend to devote to all the information I can obtain about Sunday-school work. It seems so much more important to me than ever before; his words seemed to invest it with such a dignity. After every lecture I felt as if I must get a lot of children together, and try to teach them, before I forget how.

"He showed us that, while a heart fully consecrated to Christ is the most important qualification for the work, yet that alone would never make a good teacher. A sympathy with children and knowledge of child-nature are indispensable, and he thinks these can only be obtained by patient study. He recommends such works as 'Peep of Day' and 'Line upon Line.'

"It is the business of a teacher to *instruct, please,* and *move;* and the aim of a teacher should be to make the plain, simple teaching of the Bible more clear and interesting.

"Mr. Pardee believes in a great deal of questioning, though he thinks that question books should not be used as a rule. He gave us two or three Bible lessons on Sunday, in which he gave us practical illustrations of the best modes of teaching.

"I must try and give you an outline of a 'model lesson,' taught by a young lady near London, for it was really beautiful.

"A young lady of twenty was requested to give a model of her manner of teaching, before a most intelligent audience of about five hundred persons. The children were to be picked up off the streets, and she was to meet them for the first time before the audience. The class of little boys and girls was seated in a gallery, in full view of the audience. When the young lady came in, she greeted them with a perfectly calm, cordial manner, and instead of proceeding at once to religious instruction, asked the question :—

" 'What kind of weather have you had in London lately?'

" The children simultaneously responded,"—

" 'Very rainy.'

" 'Well,' said the teacher.' " 'What is rain good for ?'

" After a pause, a little boy responded :

" 'Good to wash the streets,' to the evident amusement of the audience.

" But the wise teacher would not see the boy discouraged, and turning to him, said :

" 'That's right my boy. Multitudes of little boys and girls like you would be suffering now if the rain did not come to wash the dirty streets of London.'

"After eliciting several other replies to the question, the young lady said, ' Our lesson for this evening, is the reply of the Tyrolese woman to her son,'—' God has a plan for every man.'

" She then made them repeat it in concert, and afterwards called on a few individually, till all were perfectly familiar with the words. Then turning to one child she said,

"' Mary Ryan, where do you live ? ' and by a series of questions obtained the exact location of her home.

"' Well Mary, what is our lesson for the evening ? '

"' God has a plan for every man.'

"' What is God's plan for your father ? '

"' Nothing ma'am.'

"' Why, what does he do ?   Has'nt he any business ?'

"' No ma'am, he's only a plumber. '

"' Then Mary, that's God's plan for your father,' said she, and then went on to show how London would suffer if there were no plumbers in it.   Thus she went round the class, and coming back to Mary, explained that God had a plan for boys and girls, as well as for men.

"' Now Mary,' said she, ' what is God's plan for you ?'

"' Nothing, ma'am.'

.  "' Don't you do anything, Mary ? '

"' Yes, ma'am, I knit father's socks.'

" Then she showed her that this was God's plan for her.   She then asked a tiny little girl the same question, and received the invariable answer,

"'Nothing, ma'am.'

"' Why Carrie, what do you do when your mother is washing ? '

"' Nothing ma'am.'

"' Are you quite sure you don't do anything ? '

"' Yes ma'am.'

" ' Can't you think of anything you do, Carrie ?'

" ' I don't do anything ma'am, only *mind the baby*.'

" And then it was explained to the wondering child that this was the work given her to do. After a good deal more questioning, calculated to impress the lesson on their minds, she related the little story from which the maxim was taken.

" There was once a little Tyrolese cripple who was always complaining of his uselessness, and to his oft repeated complaints, his mother always replied, ' God has a plan for every man, and for every one there is *some* thing to do.' One day when the boy was thirteen or fourteen years of age, he wandered off to a fair, which was held near his village. He soon wearied of looking at the sports in which he could not join, and turned his face homewards. In climbing a hill, he became weary when about half way up, and lay down under a tree to rest, and soon fell asleep. When he awoke all was still, and the stars were shining down upon him. He rose and went up to the top of the hill. Here he found the signal fire built and all ready to light, but no sentinel to apply the match in case of alarm. Looking down into the valley he saw the sentinels feasting and making merry, forgetful of their neglected duty. As the boy stood looking over the quiet landscape, he saw a man rise from a distant hill, and then another, and another, till a company of French soldiers, the foes of his country, were in full view. Firmly grasping the flint, he quickly lighted the pile, and immediately from many a distant hill-top rose an answering flame, and his country was saved.

" As the boy went slowly down the mountain, he received a ball from a French musket, in the back of his neck. He lived a few days, and then died, amid the thanks of a grateful nation.

" One of our lessons was the first four verses of the eighth chapter of Matthew ; I was amused at one of his illustrations on the blackboard. He ——

"Well M., I had got so far, when I was quietly informed that I had just five minutes in which to arrange my fire for the night and place myself 'in a horizontal position between the sheets.' By the time my fire was fixed, two minutes were left, and then ensued some little ' flying round ; ' but I was'nt tardy. I had been writing steadily all the evening, without noticing the bells at all.

" ' I'll see now if I can give you that illustration.' Mr. Pardee says :—

" 'We will represent the leper on the blackboard, but not by much of a figure ; just let this straight mark represent him in a prostrate condition.

Health lost,
____   Hope-less,    " ' This' said he, ' is his condition be-
Help-less,   fore Christ comes.'
Home-less.

" He then drew another mark and rubbed out the last syllable of each word, making it stand thus :

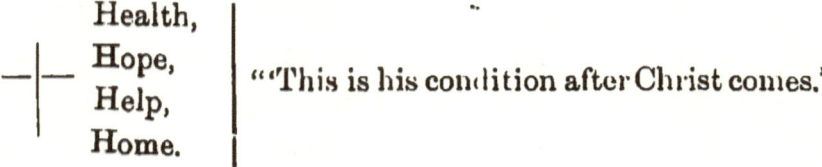

Health,
Hope,    "'This is his condition after Christ comes.'
Help,
Home.

"Jan. 24th, 1868.

"DARLING SISTER M.,

"I must send you at least a note to-morrow morning, if only to keep you in remembrance, and induce you to favor me frequently with your precious little letters. Perhaps I may get one to-night, but I do not expect it.

"I am very much interested in my studies, and do not find them very difficult. Cons. Text Book is so nice. The first day that we recited, Miss G. (who is our teacher), asked me a great many questions about our provincial form of government, as it was suggested by the lesson. Most of the questions I could answer, but felt very much afraid that I should expose my ignorance. (Oh! lovely! I've just got a letter from you, and I must stop to read it.) There, now; I've read it all. You dear child, you don't know what a feast it has been. From *home*, you know.

"I wanted to ask papa if Newfoundland is in the Dominion. I am ashamed not to know, but think it is not. Are the Governors for the Provinces appointed by the Governor-General, or by the people, or by the Executive Council, or what? And did we have any voice in the appointment of our Governors before Confederation? Papa's wisdom can answer these questions without any difficulty.

"Please send me a copy of the paper containing papa's 'statement,' *without fail,* and at once. Also that little book describing the Provincial buildings, and *everything else you think I might like.* (A modest request!)

"I'm glad to hear that you are doing so nicely in

Italian. Do you experience no inconvenience from studying? No distress in your dear little head?

"We commenced our gymnastics to-day; the class I am in is very large, numbering over seventy. They will hardly excuse any one from practising this series, and have an 'invalid class,' in which the more infirm practice together, and take the lighter exercises. A. F. is in that class, and to-day Miss E. asked all to remain, after the class was dismissed, who were troubled with their feet in any way. A. remained, and as Miss E. saw her waiting, she asked her, 'Do your feet trouble you, Miss F. ?' A. replied, in a tone of some anxiety, 'Well—not much—they're *very large*, Miss E.—they trouble me that way.' It was some time before Miss E. could recover her equilibrium sufficiently to continue her remarks. You know how she would say it.

"Do you know, M., that the fortieth Congress is the —, or that the present Congress is the fortieth? They have a new Congress every two years, whereas in England our Parliament lasts seven years. Ask papa if the Legislative, Judicial and Executive departments of Government are *separated* in our *arrangements*, as in the States.

"Well, M., I did not intend to write more than one sheet full when I commenced. This is Friday evening, and I have no composition subject yet. What *will* I take?

"You cannot write too often.

"I must say good night, though I do so reluctantly.

"Give loads of love to all, from

"Your most lovingest Sister,

"ANNIE."

"Jan. 29th, 1868.

"DARLING A.,

"I got your nice letter last night with M's, but I can only send you a few words in reply, for two reasons, one is want of time, but I am chiefly detained from writing by the uncomfortable consciousness that I sprained my right hand thumb slightly this morning, not enough to distress me except when I want to use it for writing or some such exercise. You must know, my dear, that roommate and I own the only sled in the Seminary. I felt that we did not have half enough out-door exercise, and thought we must invent some plan to induce us to stay out longer, so this idea presented itself, and I straightway went to Miss W. and asked her if she would have any objection to our coasting. Of course Miss W. was willing, and 'Prof. B.' consented to make us a sled. Now behold it! A fine structure, capable of carrying three girls, and only cost half a dollar! is on runners too. At the suggestion of Miss P., I have named it 'Eclipse,' both because it was made on the evening of the eclipse, and because I intend it to earn that high sounding title. We have a splendid place to coast, and I only wish you could go flying down the hill with me some day, only I don't want you to tumble over and sprain your poor thumb as I did.

"Well, did you all see the lunar eclipse on Wednesday evening? It was quite cloudy here, so that we could not see much through the telescope, but it looked quite plainly eclipsed without.

F

" Oh ! A., I've been puzzling my poor brain over the most distracting *logarithms* for two days ; I have trigonometry on the brain (and that's worse than influenza), but then I know it will be a delightful study some time.

" Your letters were lovely darlings.  Wish I could write to M., but time and thumb forbid.

" M. W. sent M. and me a box of 'goodies,' all the way from Pittsburg, Penn., was'nt she kind ?  It had a tin box of oysters in it ; a frosted fruit cake ; *lots* of crackers and ginger snaps, and some candy and oranges.

" Well, darling, I must say good-night.  Please give my love to all the dear people, and tell M. school closes on Friday, April 2nd, only about eight weeks more ! incredible !

" Your loving sister,

" Annie G. Johnson."

———

"Jan. 31st, 1868.

" M. Darling.,

" Your long and interesting letter came to cheer me this evening.  How busy you must be ; you will learn to improve the time as well as mamma does before long. I am trying to do a little more than usual in the letter-writing line, but it would not do for my correspondence to reach the mammoth dimensions that mamma's has gradually assumed.

" The days are filled up with an unvarying, unremitting round of duties.  Shall I give you an account of them ?

" After breakfast, I put my room in order and study

history till first recitation, which comes at half-past eight; recite history and attend devotions till a quarter before ten; come to my room and study ' Introduction to Study of the Bible' till fourth hour; recite 'Study of the Bible,' and then go to reading till dinner. After dinner study Constitutional Text Book till first hour; recite, then practice, then gymnastics, then sections and hall.

" After hall, walk and study history till supper; study same till recess-meeting; then go to recess-meeting, after that study my other two lessons till within half-an-hour before retiring bell; then go to sleep, and so on till next morning. It would be pretty hard if Wednesdays and Saturdays did not come in to vary the programme; but I love to be so busy.

" We heard from Miss Hollister to-day; she had arrived at her destination, but not without the loss of all her clothing and everything she valued. Her things were stolen by a band of mountain robbers, who seized and emptied the trunks and boxes, taking from them everything of much value. Of course, this is a great loss to her as she had prepared a supply for years to come, and cannot easily replace them in that mountain region. I believe the teachers are getting up a box of things to send out to her. I think I would have felt like *crying*.

" The 'Study of the Bible' is a work by Nicholls, intended to lead to the study of the Scriptures by showing their divine authority; the purpose for which they were given to man; the manner in which that purpose has been fulfilled; by speaking of the interpretation of the

Bible, and giving a sketch of the Jewish form of government, religion, different sects, etc. In connection with every lesson, we have to learn a good many texts of Scripture, and I think it will be very useful. It is by no means an easy study, and the book might have been written in a more interesting style.

"Roman History takes a great deal of study, but it is very interesting. Constitutional Text Book is decidedly easy, but we have such long lessons that sometimes I have hardly time to read them through once. I like Miss G. as a teacher, very well indeed; she is strict, but seems to take an interest in the study. I have been astonished lately at the great influence of exaggeration. I found that I had been dreading having to recite to Miss G. just because the girls have always given me such frightful accounts of their experience with her; and it is just so with my studies; I always expect to have a hard time with them."

"Loads of love to all at home.

"From your most loving Sister,

"ANNIE."

<hr />

"Feb. 10, 1868.

"DARLING SISTER M.,

"I have just read your letter, and also mamma's and A.'s. Why, you all seem to think I'm homesick, or *something*. What did I say to make such an impression? Well, be comforted by the assurance that I'm not homesick by any means: I have no time for such foolishness, in fact

I'm neglecting a lesson now to write this, but cannot deny myself the pleasure. Everything seems so *inexorable* that if I put off one thing to attend to another, it disarranges everything; I just tread along, doing one thing at a time, and seem unable to squeeze anything else in between my duties, except an occasional letter home.

"I have just been at 'hall;' Miss E. has been talking to us a long time about our wastefulness as a family, and really her statistics were quite alarming. At the lowest calculation, the sum of two thousand dollars is thrown away in the waste barrel every year. Just think of it. We use nine barrels of flour a week, at fifteen dollars a barrel. Three hundred pounds of butter a week at forty cents a pound, and out of that seven or eight pounds a day are thrown away. After showing us the evil of it in the most earnest manner possible, she asked all those who were willing to pledge themselves to do all in their power to prevent a continuance of this, to rise. We sprang to our feet with great alacrity, but, dear me, I wonder how long the impression will last.

"Poor Mrs. F. has a hard place, and I think she does wonders, and is remarkably amiable considering her trials.

I've often been shocked at College boys; the unfeeling, inconsiderate spirit they frequently manifest, but I don't believe after all that they are much worse than school girls. I should think our teachers would lose all patience with us sometimes, we are so unreasonable.

" I've read nothing this term except a few ' Conversations with Goethe' for sheer want of time ; I do not at all regret taking three studies, for I know I would not have had enough to do with only two. We are through with Ancient History, and will only be reviewing now till the end of the term, and that will be very easy. Constitutional Text Book is very easy for me, and so pleasant to learn.

" Miss F. has not yet returned, but I suppose she will be here next week. Her place (in her executive capacity) is very efficiently filled by Miss E. and Miss W., but we miss her much, especially at morning devotions.

" Now you must be said good-night to by your sister.

"ANNIE."

———

"Feb. 15th, 1868.

"A. DARLING,

" I must not neglect you altogether to-night, but cannot devote many minutes to you, for that inexorable bell will presently toll forth its summons to all the daughters of Holyoke to yield themselves to the influence of 'tired nature's sweet restorer,' and forget the cares and burdens of the day in 'balmy sleep.'

"How do you get on with music and Italian ? Tell me all about it, and how you like Italian by this time ; do you really manage to keep up with M. ?

"A, dear, the third Emperor of Rome was Caligula. Oh ! such a man as he was ! He was very wicked, and some things he did were so silly, that I think he must have been a little crazy. He had a favorite horse, whose name was Incitatus, and he made people pay more reverence to that horse than to any human being in the world. He built him a stable of gold with a manger of ivory, and frequently invited him to his own royal table. He was about to confer on him a very high office in the government, when the poor horse died, just in time to save the members of the government from the mortification of having a horse share their honors and duties. What do you think of him, A.?

"Bugby is beside me putting a new knob on our table drawer. He does talk so. Because we got a little rivet out of our stove, he says, 'O what girls you be to break your stoves.'

"Give loads of love to all, and write soon to your loving sister,

"ANNIE."

----

"Feb. 15th, 1868.

"DEAREST PAPA,

"I must write a note to-night in acknowledgment of your very welcome letter, containing information and suggestions of a most valuable and acceptable character.

"I called to see Miss G. this evening, and in the course of conversation told her what you said about the Privy Council; she was much interested, and said she would ask me to tell the class some day. Miss G. also spoke of her desire to obtain information about the English government, and the difficulty of obtaining such information. I have consulted all the Encyclopedias I could find, without obtaining much satisfaction; what would you advise in such a case?

"I cannot help admiring Miss G.'s general intelligence. I think she can surpass even our friend Mrs. M. in her knowledge of politics.

"I often wonder how you and other gentlemen can keep up a knowledge of everything that is going on in the political world, without spending all your time in reading the papers. When I think of commencing to inform myself in regard to such things, I am at once overwhelmed with the idea of the vast amount I would have to read before I could get such a clear idea of what *has been* going on, as to enable me to understand the events of to-day; but probably if I should make the effort it would prove to be much less difficult than it seems now.

"We are studying about the Roman Emperors now, in history; have just finished the first six Cæsars. What utterly *in*human beings they were, with one or two exceptions.

"After Caligula, Claudius and Nero, the reign of Vespasian seems so refreshing; it seems, for a moment, to lift the empire from its degradation.

"It is wonderful to trace the fulfilment of prophecy through all this history. Where we are studying now, the mighty power of the 'fourth beast,' having 'the body of the leopard, the feet of the bear, and the mouth of a lion,' is just beginning to decline. I think that a thorough knowledge of profane history enhances the interest of the Bible very much. I want very much to read the writings of Josephus, but dear me, there is so

much, oh! so much to read.  Miss H. is reading Shakespeare to us, in connection with our ancient history; of
course she cannot read much, but it is very interesting;
what a mind Shakespeare had!

> " Good-bye now.
>
> " Your loving daughter,
>
> " ANNIE G. JOHNSON."

                                        " FEB. 27, 1868.

" DEAREST PAPA,

> " Mr. Greene was regularly installed yesterday as
the pastor of our church.  The service in the afternoon
commenced at half past one, and continued till about four
o'clock.  There was singing, prayer, and singing again.

" Then Prof. Tyler, from Amherst, preached a very
long sermon in his peculiar manner, after which there
was prayer again, when another minister gave the charge
to Mr. Greene.  The charge was very interesting, and
also the speech made by the one who extended to him
the ' right hand of fellowship.'  Then followed the charge
to the people, by one who was formerly pastor of this
church.  He spoke in a plain and practical manner, telling the people that their pastor was a *man*, and not an
*angel*; warning them not to meddle with his domestic
concerns; not to expect him to visit any in their families
who were sick, unless they first informed him of the fact
that they were sick; not to complain, when he called to
see them, that it was a long time since they had seen
him, and that he was quite a stranger, but to welcome

him heartily, and show such pleasure in seeing him, and so friendly and genial a spirit, that he would be induced to come oftener. An anthem concluded the service, and Mr. Greene was our pastor.

"I suppose you are deeply interested in watching the progress of affairs at Washington. Do you get the news without much delay? Of course you know that impeachment seems inevitable now. What do you think of it? There is quite an excitement in the school about political affairs; the reading room looks quite like a beehive during recreation hours.

"And what do you think about Ireland? Do you agree with John Bright in his plans for a reformation? I mean especially in his wish to have the Romish Church receive an equal share of support from the English government as any other.

"Do you notice that, in speaking of parts of our government which especially delegate power to the people (the Privy Council for instance), you speak of it as being *Republican*; as if an approximation to that was desirable. Now, if a government is better in proportion to its *Republicanism*, why not have a complete Republic at once? Perhaps I don't understand your meaning at all, but I was a little puzzled about this, and so mentioned it for your explanation. Don't you think that the constitution is in fault, in leaving the highest offices open to all, with no regard to education? So many of the men at the head of this nation are almost entirely destitute of education and refinement also, that I should think it would have an injurious influence on society in general.

"Was there any exitement in Ottawa about the 'Papal Zouaves' who left Montreal so lately? What is the special danger of the Pope at present, that he should require so much assistance? I should like to know what you think of the movement.

"I don't understand why, in the estimate of the representation in the House of Commons, for the year 1871, the population of Nova Scotia is supposed to decrease; they calculate that Nova Scotia will then have eighteen, instead of nineteen representatives; New Brunswick remains the same, while Ontario alone increases; and, if you are not tired out with my questions; what, in the American government corresponds to our executive council? What are the powers of the ex. council; how is it appointed, and of whom is it formed?

"Oh papa dear, how will you ever manage to answer all my questions, is'nt it a great *bother*? But I wish you would sometime take this letter and write to me; I think you will find that I have suggested topics sufficient for quite a long letter.

* * *

"March 11th, 1868.

"DARLING M.,

"This is Wednesday, and we have had *our first debate*. Met at four o'clock in the lecture room. The question was, 'Is a lie ever justifiable'? Affirmative, Miss B., with F. S. as second; negative, M. H. with F. H, The argument on both sides was very good indeed, and the whole affair quite a success.  I was called on to speak, but being quite unprepared, declined.  Question was decided in the negative by an almost unanimous vote.  We are to have a  paper next  meeting instead of a debate. Editresses, A. H., M. B., and A. G. J.

"I wish you would take up the discussion of this question about 'lying' at the table sometime, and tell me the result.  Define lying, as *any attempt whatever* to *deceive*. The affirmative brought forward  this argument, Christ was one day walking with His Disciples, when He came to their place of abode, as they stopped 'He made as though He would have gone further.' They argue that this was an attempt to deceive, as Christ afterwards, on their invitation, stayed with  them all night, and must have  known that He would do so.  I'm sure I do  not know which side to take.  Where  could  we  draw  the  line?  Of course an educated conscience could readily decide in  what case it would be justifiable for *itself*, but is there no general rule that would apply?  I voted for the negative, not because I was convinced, but because that side had the greatest weight of argument.

"My room-mate and I do get into such discussions.  We have just finished one about miracles, M. taking the stand that the day of miracles had passed away, and I the opposite.  Then we are always getting unintentionally into arguments about church doctrine,—M. is a grand one to argue with, and I think it tends to our mutual enlightenment.  Table conversation  is quite brisk these eventful times.

" M. is reading Cicero on the Immortality of the soul ; it sounds perfectly ridiculous in parts, 'For I think this to be more miserable, not to be, when you have been." ' Then those who are not born are already miserable because they are not.'

" You must tell me the result of the 'important day in the Government' when you write. I am so glad you have become acquainted with and like Lady H.—but I must stop at once.

" Good-bye,

" ANNIE."

————

" March 16th, 1868.

" M. DEAR,

"I was very glad to receive your letter last night and will try and get a note written to-night as I have a little time now before the retiring bell will ring.

"I will, in the first place, make a suggestion. I have found it a most convenient plan to take care of my letters by having a pasteboard box for that special purpose, and whenever I receive a letter I write on the end of the envelope the date of its reception and put it with the others inside a rubber band, and then in the box. It is more convenient to keep each letter in its own envelope. I mention this because I remember the 'times' we often have at home to find letters just when we want them, and I think if you were to keep a box on your table and always put them right in that, it would save much time and trouble.

"Really, M., you wax eloquent when you get on a theme so near your *heart-strings* as the one dilated upon in your last letter. You little Radical! I don't know what to say to you. You know you always did dash ahead of me in admiration and praise of our institutions, and in opposition to those of the United States. Nevertheless, I do not go as far as T. does, by any means. With you, I can say, 'I'm a British subject, and am thankful and delighted that I am,' but I think that the best way to shew our patriotism is to be ourselves an honor to our country, and to contribute our mite of influence towards those improvements which will make our country such as we wish it to be. Wait till we get up that model school, now existing in the realm of the future.

> " I wait for the day when dear hearts shall discover,
>    While dear hands are laid on my head,—
> ' The child is a woman, the book may close over,
>    For all the lessons are said.' "

" But I'm in no hurry for this blissful consummation; study is delightful, except for the fact that every ray of light penetrating my cranium, seems only to disclose darker *caverns* of ignorance to be filled with the illuminations of science. (Oh!!)

"Spring has come, and with it the dread intelligence that travellers from South Hadley must depart via Willymansett. School closes a week from Tuesday: bills handed in this week.

"The retiring bell warns me with relentless tone that I must close the labors and duties of the day, and say a reluctant good-night to all you darling ones at home.

"Did I acknowledge the receipt of the papers Papa sent me?

"Why doesn't my pet A. write?

"Good-night, darling.

"Your

"ANNIE."

---

"March 18th, 1868.

"MON CHER PERE,

"I think I told you that the trustees had appealed to the Legislature for a grant of $40.000; well, the claim was refused a hearing, but Mr. Durant made some new arrangement, and sent for Miss French to come to Boston and present the claims of the Seminary. So Misses French and Evans went yesterday, and we hope they will be successful.

"I hear that there is being founded in England a college for ladies, on a scale as liberal as Oxford and Cambridge; giving ladies equal advantages with the students at those colleges; isn't that grand? An example that is worthy to be followed by every nation.

"I'm so glad that I will have an opportunity of visiting the cabinet at Amherst College; it is a finer one than is possessed by any other college in the State. I am reading over Hitchcock's Geology now, so that I may profit by seeing the cabinet, more than I otherwise would.

"Studies are over, but we have before us the dreadful ordeal of examinations. I am examined in Analysis on

Tuesday morning; Constitution on Wednesday morning; Study of the Bible Wed. afternoon, and Ancient History Thursday morning. I have very little fear about failing in the examinations, and so feel quite a relief in the fact that recitations are over.

"For next term, think I will take Botany, and perhaps Physiology or Geology. Do you know anything about Mr. Papineau in Canada? He is evidently very anxious to bring about that union of the Provinces with the United States, which the *Tribune* says is the 'glorious destiny' of all British America. There is a quotation in the *Tribune* from a lecture delivered by him, and he seems to be a prominent man in Canada.

"You will probably find my letters quite short and uninteresting till examinations are over; if I fail, I'll say nothing about them, but if I do well, you will probably hear about it.

"Your loving daughter,

"ANNIE G. JOHNSON."

---

"March, 1868.

"We have with us at present, Mr. Foote, connected with the 'Howard Mission' in New York city. He spoke to us in the sem. on Friday evening, and in the church on Sunday, giving us an account of the founding of the mission, its work, and the manner in which it is supported.

"Mr. Van Meter is at the head of the institution; the object is to gather together the neglected children of the city, and feed, clothe and instruct them. There are now six hundred and fifty in the school, and of these, five hundred and fifty get no meal except the dinner of soup and bread at the 'home.' Six hours are devoted to instruction, and then they return to their homes.

"When the parents are willing, they place the children in Christian homes to be brought up; and I believe about a thousand have already been provided for in this way.

"It is hard to believe that such misery exists as has been described to us by Mr. Foote. Just think of *ten thousand* people walking the streets of New York every night, unable to find a shelter, even in the station houses. These station houses are filled every night, and to the station master, the managers of the mission give tickets for distribution among these poor starving beings, stating that bread, butter and coffee can be obtained at the mission rooms on Sunday mornings. Now, about two hundred assemble at the appointed time, and when they have fully satisfied their hunger, they are exhorted by these earnest men to come to Christ. Of course very few are ever present more than once, but at every meeting the efforts are rewarded by the knowledge that some have then commenced a new life. The cost of a Sunday morning breakfast is ten dollars. By providing this they must reach a class of people who would otherwise be totally neglected.

"Mr. Foote's object in coming here now is to raise funds for the mission. They expend a hundred dollars a week, and are supported entirely by voluntary contributions."

G

"March 24th, 1868.

" DARLING M.,

"A new name for Mt. Hol. Sem.,—christening by Mr. F., of Howard Mission—'Dove's Nest,' is quite cast in the shade by the 'Half-way house between heaven and earth.'

"I was examined in Analysis this morning ; of course I didn't fail in that little thing, but the worst are to come yet.    I don't intend to distress myself about them at all, for that would only increase my liability to fail.    So far the examinations have been very creditable, but they are no test of scholarship ; some of the best scholars failed utterly to-day.    I expect Mr. G. will be in to-morrow, and I am told he asks lots of questions."

---

## IV.

### 1868.

" AMHERST, March 31st, 1868.

" DARLING MINIBUS,

"I don't believe I have told you the result of my examinations. Well, I was so fortunate as not to fail in one; not even the shadow of a failure.

" Thursday afternoon examinations closed, and Mary and I started out for a walk, intending to go about two miles to engage a man to take us over to Amherst on Saturday. The man's house was away up among the hills, and after accomplishing our business, we started straight across the hills to find Mr. M's house, in order to call. Coming to a deep, rapid stream, we wandered up and down searching for a place narrow enough to cross, but finding none, we climbed a hill and dragged down two great rails from a fence and erected a bridge for ourselves, on which we crossed with great ease. On we wandered, over hills and through fields, climbing fences, and sinking ankle-deep in swamps, still finding no trace of Mr. M's.

" Bye and bye, we came to a mill which we determined to explore; there were several women in it, making cloth and flannel, and they kindly explained everything to us.

Warned by the setting sun, we again started on our search, and at last, almost tired out, found the house, after a tramp of three miles over the hills. It was getting quite dark and we only remained long enough to say a few words and get our pockets filled with apples, then took up our weary march for the Sem., two miles distant. Oh! how tired we were, but we got there before eight o'clock and had a comfortable supper. The next day locomotion was attended with serious difficulty, and it was not till Saturday that we regained our usual grace of motion.

" Saturday afternoon we had a pleasant drive across the mountains, and reached Mrs. W's. just at tea-time.

" To-morrow I expect to go and see the College cabinets. I anticipate quite a treat; then we are going soon to see the Agricultural College, which has been lately established here. On the whole I think we will have a pleasant vacation."

―――――

" AMHERST, Mass., April 10th, 1868.

" MINE OWN ONE,

" Do you have such weather as this in Ottawa ? Old Winter, provoked at the joy with which we hailed his departure, has returned to us, and bids fair to prolong his stay.

" Let me tell you M., I have heard Parepa ! There was a grand concert last night in Springfield, and Mr. W.

very kindly urged me to go over with him ; so we started
at four o'clock ; got to Northampton in time to take the
five o'clock train, and were in Springfield before six
o'clock.    We got supper at a hotel, and went to the Hall
at seven.    The concert was in the City Hall, which is said
to be the first in Massachusetts ; seats three thousand
people.    Before eight o'clock the Hall was full.    Mr. W.
was unable to secure a reserved seat, but we obtained a
very good one.    At eight o'clock it was announced to us
that by some oversight all the music had been left in Hart-
ford and could not be on hand till the half-past eight
train, however the concert commenced before nine.    There
was a choir of sixty singers, and an orchestra of sixteen
instruments.    They sang Haydn's Oratorio of the Creation ;
you remember that is what we sing at school this year,
and you may be sure I was interested.    There are a great
many solos, both soprano, tenor, and bass, in the Oratorio.
Parepa represented Gabriel, and two gentlemen, Uriel and
Raphael.    There was one piano, a violin, violincello, and
two bass viols, a flute, French horn, trombone, and
several other instruments of music.    And oh ! they *did*
make music ! Such a musical feast I never enjoyed before.
I was just *satisfied* with everything.    Parepa came on to
the stage, dressed in a light green satin, with diamonds
flashing from her head and neck, and a scrap of elegant
lace suspended by a chain from her finger, to represent a
handkerchief.    She could hardly be called pretty, and yet
she has such a bright, unaffected manner that she seems
like a cunning little girl ; she is about medium height and

quite stout ; looks like her pictures, only they don't give
her expression at all.  She sang  with spirit and feeling.
On upper C, her voice rang  out  through  two or three
measures with the most unwavering clearness, and at the
end of the last chorus she threw her sweet voice up  to D,
and sustained it for some  time.  It  was  the  last note I
heard her sing  and  it  seems  as  if  I could  hear it now.
How I wished that you could  have  been there.  This is
the first Oratorio I have heard  really *sung*, but I hope it
will not be the  last.

"It was after eleven when we came away, but the evening had been all too short.  Carl Rosa, Parepa's husband,
conducted the concert.

"We went back to the hotel and got our wrappings and
took the train for Northampton ; then we had a long, cold
drive to Amherst, and found ourselves in Mrs. W's parlor
at two o'clock.  Everyone was in  bed of course, but they
had left a supper for us,  and  we  sat down and got nice
and warm, and before three I went  to my room to sleep
till ten this morning.

" On enquiring for letters, F. produced yours from his
letter box where he had been hoarding it up for me.

" Yes, I read the  account of  that assassination in the
*Springfield Republican* some  days  ago,  and  conclude
that it has made a great excitement in Ottawa.  I shall
want to hear  all  about  it.  What  a  frightful thing  it
was. *

"I have been, as yet, only to one  of the cabinets and the

---

* Assassination of Hon. Thos. D'Arcy McGee.

conservatory. The first thing that greeted my eyes on going into the cabinet was the skeleton of a most monstrous animal, belonging to a species long since extinct. Near it was the skeleton of a whale's head ; the interior of which a gentleman informed me was a very pleasant place to study, when you wish to be alone. I was accompanied by one of the Amherst Seniors, who facetiously remarked that he could truly say he would be happy to answer all questions as far as he could, but before he had gone far, I became convinced that his knowledge was hardly superior to mine ; and so, for lack of information I failed to appreciate everything as I wished to. I saw the frightful Gorilla with the broken gun in its paws, it made me shudder.

" Well, I can give you no idea of the extent and variety of this vast collection, but I intend to see much more before school commences. The conservatory is very fine, and will be improved. I have played a great deal to-day, and as it has been trying Oratorios for Mr. O., I'm pretty tired, for that is certainly most tiresome music to play, I have to fix my attention so closely.

" The people in this house do everything they can to make our vacation pleasant.

" To-morrow I'm going to try and learn to ride on horseback, on A's horse ; won't that be splendid.

" The snow is a foot deep on the ground, and this is April.

" I thought I would send Mamma this white bow for her neck. I made it after being told how by a lady. Quite simple, but useful.

"How does Ottawa get on ?  my papers have not been sent to me from the Seminary, this vacation.

" It waxes late, and I am tired after last night's dissipation ; will you excuse me now ?

" Your loving Sister,<br>
" Annie G. Johnson."

———

" April 15th, 1868.

" M. Darling.

"This last vacation day finds me still at Amherst, and expecting to stay here for a day or two longer.

" Day after day I have been confidently expecting my face to be better,* and when I awoke yesterday morning to find it still growing worse, I felt well-nigh discouraged and almost overcome by homesickness.  I did not get up till after dinner, and then lay on the sofa most of the afternoon and evening.  The inflammation seems to have settled in my lips, and they are very sore indeed, though better to-day than yesterday.  I thought it would be better for me to remain here till Saturday than to go to the Seminary and be shut up in my room all the time. Mr. W. is going to borrow some books for me, so that I can study and not get behind my classes.

" On Tuesday morning Alice put her side saddle on the horse, and I dressed myself in her riding habit and a thick veil, and took my first riding lesson.  I always knew I could ride if only I could get on a horse.  I rode

---

* Alluding to a swelling of the face brought on by a drive in a snow-storm.

about near and around the house ; at first only venturing
on a modest walk, but growing bolder, essayed to make
the horse gallop. Not being much accustomed to a saddle
he would gallop a few steps, making me feel as easy and
secure as if in a rocking-chair, but his gallop would
merge into a trot which pounced me up and down in a
most unedifying manner."

---

"FRIDAY AFTERNOON.

"To-day my face is better, though my looks are not at
all improved, probably will not be for about two weeks.
I have just been fixing my hair, and positively, though
all alone, I had to stop and laugh at my own face; but
alas ! a great trial is, that I cannot laugh without the
greatest discomfort. If you want to see how I look, take
a fish and rub its scales the wrong way.

"This charming day I rebelled against staying in the
house any longer, so I went out and had a most splendid
horseback ride all alone, with two thicknesses of veil
over my physiognomy. I explored the town and its
suburbs, stopping for some time to gaze at the beautiful view from Mt. Pleasant. When I came home just
before dinner, I told Alice that I had had my heart's desire, a real horseback ride. Oh ! you don't know how
charming it is ; and when I go home in the summer we
will get a horse and you shall learn. Every one says I
ride surprisingly well for a beginner. I am talking
about myself all the time, but cannot think of anything

else, at least anything so deeply interesting. I must stop soon and prepare to go to the gymnasium and see the students practice; of course accompanied by my double veil.

"Have been reading Cicero this afternoon and think I shall like it much. Mr. O. has been feeding me on chocolate candy, and from other sources I get figs and oranges; this is the first day that I have been able to eat with any comfort, consequently my appetite has had an opportunity of becoming developed.

"On reading over my letter I see a melancholy strain about home sickness; now I charge you, heed it not; I am all over such nonsense, and feel like another person to-day; all I wanted was fresh air and exercise.

"This must be a lovely town in summer. There are a great many very handsome residences, as well as public buildings. I'm waiting anxiously to hear some Ottawa news; now mind, I must have a letter to-night without fail. Blessings on the post office ! !

"Yours, with a very great amount of love to all my fair friends, and injunctions never to undervalue their good looks.

"ANNIE JOHNSON."

"After April 15th, 1868.

"A. PET,

"If you knew how glad I was to receive your letter, and how I enjoyed reading it, I think you would speedily afford me a similar treat.

"I must tell you about my last horseback ride. It was on Tuesday morning, and made my third ride in eighteen years. Alice borrowed a beautiful little horse, spirited and excitable, for herself, and I took her larger and more staid animal; however, before we had gone very far, we came to a convenient spot for dismounting, and exchanged horses; then, if we didn't race and gallop! We were going away out to the 'Orient' for May flowers; when we were near the Orient House we stopped to let our horses drink, but when we wanted to go on my fractious little pony could not be induced to go past the corner to which we had come. All the stratagems I could think of only resulted in a disarranged harness, and we rode up to the hotel (the only house in that region), to have this made right. On our explaining our perplexities, the waiter offered to lead my horse round the corner, and so we got over that difficulty.

"Before twelve we had our baskets filled with fragrant May-flowers, and commenced a ride round the beautiful hill and valley called the Orient. Our path was narrow and winding. On one side the steep hillside formed our wall, and on the other we looked down into the lovely valley, with a crystal stream gliding through it. But I think my horse must have been deficient in the æsthetic sense (at least I *think* that big word means a love for the beautiful), for, instead of being charmed with the beauty of the scene, he only evinced a foolish terror at his elevated position, and I was obliged to dismount and lead him till his fears were calmed; but at every little bridge or unusual steepness in the path, the silly little creature would stop and obstinately refuse to proceed, so that I had to mount and dismount nearly a dozen times before we got out to the road again.

"Once on the road, our horses seemed to know that they were going home and acted in the most exemplary manner.

"We had just got into the centre of the town, and were riding quite rapidly, when I felt my saddle turning round and taking me with it. I attempted to grasp the reins, which I had been holding quite loosely, but only succeeded in tightening one, which sent my horse spinning round in a manner most uncomfortable to his rider. Seeing the state of affairs, a clerk ran out of a store near by and stopped my horse, while I sprang off and waited to have my saddle tightened; then we proceeded homewards on a delightful gallop.

"Well, dear, was that story long enough? I must stop now, for I have not a minute more time to spare.

"Write very soon again, my darling, to

"Your loving Sister,

"ANNIE."

————

"April 24th, 1868.

"MY DARLING M.,

"Being too tired and sleepy to do anything else, I concluded to talk with you a little while, instead of retiring at eight o'clock.

"Yesterday was moving day, and in this fact you will easily see a reason for my weariness. I've been trying to study Cicero, but concluded not to waste any more time in holding my book and yawning at it. We are now comfortably located in No. 100, just two rooms from old 93 which we first occupied in this building; second story, north wing; outside room. It feels and looks so cosy tonight, with a bright wood fire, while the cold wind is howling outside.

―――――

" Saturday.

" To-night I am reminded of my duty by the receipt of letters from you and A. How glad I was to get them ! You pets ; I've been laughing ever since, whenever I thought of them. I am much interested in your friend J. What I am losing by being at school all this time.

" How delighted you must be to think that E. is coming home. I suppose he must be with you now ; if so, tell him he must write to me immediately. I want to know how he likes Ottawa ; how he left T. (though I have heard from him quite lately), and also how his own health is.

" We had another snow storm yesterday ; happily it was neither very long nor very severe. Strange, strange weather for April ; but Professor Seely predicted it.

" I wish you were studying Botany. This is just the right time of year to commence, when vegetation is beginning to appear. If you should find any curiosity in a *floral* way, won't you press it and send it to me to analyse ? I'm going to try and get through my Botany in one series, as the text work is very easy. Oh, it's a charming study, and when I go home we will all have to analyse, and *perhaps* write a flora of the Ottawa country. A *flora*, you must know, is an account of the flowers of any particular section of country.

"If I think of it, I'll put a photograph of ' uncle T.' in this letter, to let you see what he looks like. I think he thinks as much of me, as if he were really my uncle ; he did everything he could to make my stay in Amherst pleasant.

" Thanks for the correction of my absurd mistake. I always mean to thank anybody after this for such correction, for I earned some commendation in vacation for so doing. One night I was playing a piece of music, new to me, for Mr. W. had made a mistake in the time, which I repeated each time I went over the piece. Mr. O. was in the room overhead, and soon he appeared in the parlor, and rather timidly pointed out my mistake, speedily making his way to the door again, fearing I suppose that he may have offended me, but I hastened to express my thanks very cordially for the trouble he had taken. The next day Mrs. W. told me that in talking to her, he had contrasted the 'lady-like manner in which I accepted his correction,' with the conduct of some young ladies under the same circumstances. Let this, my dear child, be a lesson for you through life ; follow my noble example, and may you win as precious a reward !

"How I should love to form one of your dear little Bible class ; tell me what subjects you are studying, and I will join you as nearly as five hundred miles distance, and the post office arrangements will allow.

" Is Mr. M. a Professor of music ?  Won't you delight in taking lessons again ?  It would be a nice plan for you whenever you get a piece of music, to find out all you can about the composer, and the circumstances under  which the piece was composed. I'm afraid we are rather ignorant about the theory of music.

" I must leave myself time to write a note to A.

"  Good bye, my sweet Sister,

"  ANNIE G. JOHNSON."

———

"  May 2nd, 1868.

" M. DARLING,

"  Yours of Tuesday was  received last evening, and with amusement I read  your  profuse  apologies  for not writing more frequently.  What would many of the girls here say, who hear from home but once a fortnight, if they heard you distressing yourself because you don't always write twice or three times a week.

" The idea  of mamma  thinking of sending  for me to come home.   Why I was hardly ill ; at least, it would have taken something more than that to make me give up and go home.  I expect  now that  when  I go home in the summer I will be as well as when I commenced the year. You know it is part of my daily duty now to study the ' book of Nature,' and my  botanical  researches  must be. conducive to health.

"What bright anticipations Mr. H. must have of his contemplated tour. Surely he will go to Italy. My heart's desire is to visit Greece, Classic Greece! To see the ruins of Athens—think of it: but how much pleasanter if we could visit these monuments of past greatness, undisturbed by the desecrating presence of man, and all the trifling concerns of ordinary life. I am so glad you know as much about Italian as you do. Can you read and translate it pretty easily?

"I congratulate E. on his grand discovery; I suppose I shall not dare to open my mouth when I go home for fear of some satirical criticism from his *Dominical* majesty. However, if he improves you very materially in the Grammar department, I promise him a professorship in my Seminary, *when I have one!* In consequence of the very contradictory accounts I receive, I shall have to wait and decide for myself on the color of his whiskers.

"A professor from Yale is coming to give us a course of lectures on Zoology; there are to be about twelve lectures, and we are required to attend.

" Your loving

" ANNIE."

" May 8, 1868.

" MY BELOVED SISTER,

"Having just completed the analytical examination of a member of the Order Compositæ, genus Taraxicum, species Deus-leonis, namely, a *dandelion*, I 'feel to' write to you. If you have any objection, please tell me before I go farther. I think I mentioned to you that

we expected a gentleman to give us a course of lectures
on Zoology.    He, Prof. Ebell, has come, and already given
us four lectures, which have been very interesting.    He
shows an almost boyish enthusiasm in his subject.    In
order to make the instruction more practical he proposed
excursions, called by the girls 'bugging excursions,' to
hunt for specimens of the animal life he explains in his
lectures.

"I wish you could have glanced from my window when
the first party started on such an expedition.    There
must have been nearly a hundred girls, almost all in gymnastic suits.    They went down the walk towards the
brook, two by two, headed by Miss S. and Driver.    With
their banners, consisting of white muslin nets erected on
poles waving in the air, and the Professor dashing here
and there along the lines, like a general exercising a careful supervision over his troops, they looked like a merry
little army going gaily out to battle.    Only the Seniors
and the Natural History classes went that time, but yesterday any one was invited to go who was disengaged
between ten o'clock and dinner-time.    Alas, for me! my
Botany came at ten, and I thought that would make it
impossible for me to go, till I remembered that another
class recited in the afternoon, and speedily got permission
to recite then.    How funny I looked in my gymnastic
dress, with my black cloak longer behind than my skirt,
for it was a cold, cloudy morning.    Just as we started, a
heavy shower came on; but cheered on by the Professor
we determined not to be discouraged by such a circum-

H

stance, and dashed on, over fences and rickety bridges, till we came to a flour mill, which we invaded, much to the astonishment and perplexity of the white-robed mill-men.    Here we waited till the rain had abated, when we again sallied forth, bearing with us many a floury token of our visit.  C. M. was my company—she is a sweet girl, the best member of the Senior class I believe, and I should not wonder if she should be 'Class President.'

"We were following the stream in its wanderings through the meadows, and we came to a spot where it was bridged by a log about ten yards long.  C. and I were ahead of the others, and were very anxious to try and walk across, but waited till the others came up, when the Professor himself made the trial, and then asked if any would like to try it, saying that he would help any one who might.  We saw no fun in being helped, so refused, but some others immediately undertook the hazardous journey.  Three had safely crossed, and the Professor was leading the fourth when, lo! he lost his balance and became partially submerged in the water, much to the amusement of the spectators; his equanimity apparently undisturbed, he regained his footing and proceeded on his perilous way.  We had gone about half a mile further, when glancing across the stream, we saw that the three girls who had remained on the other side after crossing the log, had arrived at the *land's end*, and could go no farther on that side.  Considerable delay was occasioned by this, as a part of the stream which was comparatively narrow had to be reached, and here they were assisted across.

" We did have a splendid time altogether.  Quite a storm of hail and rain came on as we started for home, and to crown all Miss T. sprained her ankle in climbing a fence ; but these mishaps only added zest to our enjoyment, and probably our appetites too, for I'm sure I at least did ample justice to the repast waiting for us when we got back.  If we do not obtain a great deal of scientific knowledge from these rambles, they will at least benefit our health.  Last night we had a lecture in the Gymnasium illustrated by a magic lantern, the white wall over the platform serving for a screen."

" Monday Eve.

" Yesterday brought me your letter, M., and as I read your ' eulogy ' of my letters, my thoughts went back over the long list of hurried, uninteresting epistles I have been sending you this year, and I could not but hope that you would take none of them for a ' model.'  I am glad you made that resolution (to take more pains in your own writing), for, though your letters are written in a style far above mediocrity, yet I think you seldom take time to do yourself justice.

" What a splendid time you must have had listening to so many celebrities.  Did you meet Dr. T., or did he call to see mamma ?  The Crystal Palace Concert, of which he told you, must have been something overpowering. I am afraid the day is still far off when, in Canada, we can hear an Oratorio as well performed, and before an audience as generally appreciative, as we may almost any time in *plebeian* New England.

"I am very busy this term ; more so with only two studies than last term with three, but it is a more healthy kind of business, as I have to be out of doors so much. Yesterday I analysed my thirty-sixth flower, and pressed several.                              " Your Loving-est

"ANNIE."

———

"May 11th, 1868.

" A. MY DARLING,

"Your long letter certainly deserves a speedy answer, and I only wish that I could send you one equally long and interesting.

"We have been eating some delicious oranges to-day, and I wished I could send you some of them. They were part of a dozen which Mr. W. sent to us by A., who called to see us on Friday with Mr. ———. We had a very pleasant time. Mr. ——— expressed himself as very anxious to hear some music, so we went down to the Sem-Hall, and I played a good while. They went away during supper. As we were going down the steep breakneck front stairs to the door, M. and Mr. ——— were a little ahead of us, about a third of the way down stairs. Suddenly, to our horror Mr. ——— commenced a series of gymnastic performances, quite unheard of in Miss E's vocabulary. A wild leap first to one side, then to the other, a vague, terrified grasping at invisible objects for support, and then one grand final evolution, ending in a crash, well calculated to make us tremble for the floor, had not our sympathies been enlisted on behalf of the performer, who, however, to our amazement was found at the foot of the stairway, 'right side up,' and unhurt, saving a pretty severe rap on his *vanity bump*, from which we hope he soon recovered. (If you don't understand all the big words, M. will explain, but you use such large ones yourself, that I think you will have no difficulty.) Miss E. was just giving out the hymn for devotions, when Mr. —— thumped on to the floor overhead, and she stopped in amazement, while an audible smile went round the room. The scene is present to my mind, whenever gravity seems peculiarly appropriate.

" I'm so glad you are going to have a flower garden; mind and have a pretty one ; and remember when you get your seeds, that each one contains a tiny root, stem, and almost always a pair of leaves. The first two little leaves that come up are seed-leaves, or cotyledons, as the Botany calls them. Watch your flowers and see how much you can learn about them.

" My dear, is i a favorite letter of yours ? I notice that you let it creep into e's place very often ; such partiality leads to very undesirable results in spelling.

" You know, I suppose, that pearls are found in oyster shells, but do you know how they are made. They are at first just little grains of sand, which have got into the shell, and as they irritate the oyster, it gives them a coating of some oily material, and then another and another till they become at last beautiful, round white pearls.

" I'm glad you like Algebra. You must study hard, dear, and see how much you'll know when I come home in vacation.

" When is Papa going (or coming) away ? He had better not try to surprise me if he expects to come, for I might be off on a botanizing expedition, or something of the kind, and besides, it's nice to have the anticipation.

" Now, darling, I must say good-bye, for it's almost mail time. Write again soon to

" Your loving Sister,

" ANNIE."

---

" May 21st, 1868.

" MY DARLING A.,

" Shall I waive ceremony *for once* (?) and write to you before receiving an answer to my last.

" This is a dull, rainy evening, and I have become so tired studying and sewing that I want to refresh myself by a chat with somebody.

" I have been very busy to-day pressing and analysing flowers.

" Do you want to know how to press flowers nicely ? If I were you and M. I think I would explore every *ex-plorable* region of the country round about, and gather the spring flowers as they come ; then get two square pieces of board and a large heavy stone. For myself, I went to the paper mill and bought five pounds of coarse wrapping paper in which to dry my flowers. What I got was in very large sheets, and these I folded up in several thicknesses of about a foot square, and cut single pieces of about the same size for putting the flowers in, preparatory to pressing them. The flowers ought not to be uncovered for about a week, but the drying papers should be changed every day. The sheets in which you first put them should be just like this sheet of paper, only larger, and the paper must be such as will absorb moisture readily.

"Let not E. think it beneath his dignity to share your rambles; for his benefit I will call them scientific investigations, and trust that you will have an herbarium second only to mine, when I return home. It is a phenomenon if the suburbs of Ottawa are entirely destitute of flowers. Wild flowers are far more interesting to a botanist than those that are cultivated; my botany calls some of the cultivated species *monstrosities*.

"I want to tell you about a lovely little concert we had on Tuesday afternoon. Mr. Foote, of Howard Mission, came here with six of his little ' wanderers,' in order, I suppose, to more thoroughly enlist our sympathies in their behalf, and in the afternoon brought them into the hall to sing to us. The eldest was about thirteen; she had a remarkable voice, beautifully sweet and clear, and harmonizing well with the rich alto of the little one next to her. The others sang well for such very wee children, but their actions interested me more than their singing. The poor little creatures had never been out of New York city before, and were just brimming over with delight at the novelty of everything about them. They were comfortably dressed, and we could not fully appreciate their happiness till Mr. Foote told us what homes they came from. One chubby-faced merry little thing had her home in a single underground room lighted by four small panes of glass, with a drunken father and mother, six brothers and sisters, and *two boarders !* Mr. Foote suggested that if we were dissatisfied with our board here, we might be accommodated there. Three of the children had never stepped on green grass before, and the 'cars,' 'cows,' 'chickens,' and 'green grass' filled them with unbounded delight.

"Innocent little Emma exclaimed one day, 'Oh, I'd like to come to this school a great deal better than to stay in New York.' When asked why, she answered, 'Because there's so much grass here !'

"The little creatures went away to finish their tour yesterday. Mr. Foote takes them with him, thinking truly that their childish voices will plead the cause of the mission more effectively than words of his can do.

"Again does that retiring bell—brazen bell!—sound forth its grim mandate—No! Oh, delightful ! I find it is only the half hour before retiring, so I can talk a little longer.

"So you 'take an interest' in my room-mate May, do you ? I told her that, and I think it has awakened a similar feeling in her, for she particularly desires me to give you her love.

Mr. H.'s suggestion about visiting Greece was a good one, and I shall certainly remember it with favor ; meantime, if he is in a hurry to get there, he will have a good opportunity to emulate Job's characteristic. (That's for M.)

" 'Tis sweet to be remembered," thought I, when M. made the remarks upon the subject. A. dear, try and write soon and tell me how E. is (as I *must* take second-hand news about him and his concerns)—how everybody and everything in Ottawa is progressing, 'imprimis,' the garden and fountain. I've enjoyed scribbling this very much, and only wish it were a little more legible, for I know you do not like to decipher indistinct writing.

" The *real* retiring bell has rung now, and I must say good night, and God bless my darling sister.

" Yours most lovingly,

" ANNIE."

---

" WEDNESDAY, May, 1868.

" M. DEAR,

"Such busy times as we do have this term. Prof. Ebell is here yet and this morning took all the teachers, *en masse*, on an exhibition to East Hampton and the lead mines. They returned this afternoon in a rain storm.

" I must inform you that I am a member of the Eighteenth Chapter of the 'Dana Natural History Society.' The branch with which I am connected is called the 'Mt. Holyoke Dana Natural History Society.' I think the whole affair originated with Prof. Ebell, and he has been forming ' Chapters' in the various places where he has lectured. It is composed entirely of ladies, though we have made the Professor an honorary member, in consideration of his valuable services. The object is not to make new discoveries, or additions to the field of science, but to promote a more general and practical knowledge of the Natural World. The regular meetings are to be annual, in the last week of June, but we can at any time appoint irregular meetings, and have them as frequently as we wish. This is by no means an exclusively school affair, though Miss S. is president and one or two other offices are filled by teachers ; but our connection with it continues after we leave school, and it is hoped that our interest will not be diminished. We had a meeting to-day in which the constitution was read and ratified, after some interesting debate on the various items. Prof. Ebell is the correspondent for the whole Society, to keep each Chapter apprised of the welfare and progress of the others, and sometime there is to be a general convocation of the whole. Like the Christian Association, this is to be extended into Canada, and in other ways is to be conducted like that society.

" You must be a member some day, and then we will overcome our repugnance to all *insectians* which we indiscriminately term *bugs*, and have a fine collection of our own. I will have to write to the Corresponding Secretary once every year in order to continue my connection with the Society.

———

" THURSDAY EVE.

" We have got our forty thousand dollars, and are to have an illumination this evening ! There will be a stroke of the bell five minutes after recess meeting, when we are to put lamps in our windows, and go out of doors, where we may remain till a quarter of nine when we are simultaneously to 'extinguish the illumination.'

"Miss F. read us some letters written to her by members of the State Senate, informing us that the bill for the appropriation had been sent to the Governor for his signature, which he had already promised, so that we consider *our*selves in possession of the vast treasure.

"One hour later.—The affair is all over and I am quietly settled in my room. Well, M., it was beautiful. Every window had at least two lamps in it, and when you consider the size of the building, and the regularity in the arrangement of the windows, you may have a little idea of it. Of course the town came out to see the sight, but it was quite an orderly affair.

"Prof. E. gathered us around him, directly opposite the main building, and there commenced the musical part of the entertainment. We sang 'Star Spangled Banner,' 'America,' 'Home, Sweet Home,' and other familiar airs; the Professor then proposed three cheers for the legislature of Mass. Oh! such screeching as proceeded from the untutored voices ; but it was, at least, hearty. The next proposition was to go and serenade Miss French, who had gone into the house, and round we went to her window ; here we sang 'Music in the Air,' and closed with the Doxology, as the bell summoned us to our rooms.

"Dear me, there is the retiring bell, and I will have to finish this in a hurry to-morrow morning,

" I have now analysed forty-five flowers ; five more will complete one quarter of the required number.

" Good morning M., I am going off on a zoological expedition this morning and must get ready very soon. We have only one more lecture to hear.

" This was a glorious morning, but the sunshine has gone, and there is a prospect of rain.

" Give much love to all at home, from

"Yours lovingly,

. "ANNIE."

---

" May 28th, 1868.

" DARLING M.,

" At the weary close of a busy, excited day, I must sit down and try and bring my mind into that state of equilibrium requisite to enable me intelligently to recount all that has happened.

" At five o'clock this morning I shook the sleep from my heavy eyelids, and spent the morning till breakfast time in getting affairs in order for the day. After breakfast I was coming through the dining-hall, when May, with the appearance and effect of a small whirlwind, came rushing toward me, exclaiming, incoherently, ' What *do* you suppose has happened ?' As soon as my bewildered senses had grasped the truth that Papa was really in the reception room, I sped thither with the speed which only *such* a motive could induce. But, oh ! the amazement and delight when I really saw Papa before me, I need not attempt to tell you how I felt ; you all, M.

especially, can fill up the outline, with its brilliant col-
ouring.

"Of course I must bring Papa to my room, so I apprised May of my intention and got permission of Miss W.

"Then Papa went to the stable and engaged a horse
and carriage to take us down to the South Hadley Falls.
It was about nine o'clock when we started, and we had a
delightful drive, and then a very interesting time examin-
ing the paper mills. None of us had ever been in a
paper mill before, and we followed the process of making
the paper from the very beginning in the rag-room to the
last, where the smooth white sheets were prepared for
sale. Some time when I have more time I may tell you
all about it. We got back to the Seminary about an
hour before dinner. Papa persisted in taking his dinner
at the hotel instead of here, and about one o'clock came
back and I got Miss N. to go over the house with us.
We saw everything there was to see, and Papa seemed
much pleased with the arrangements.

"After this we went to the south music room, and I
played for Papa, and after a short time got A. H. to come
in and make Papa's acquaintance.

"The rest of the time we went out on the grounds and
remained till the stage came and took Papa from my
sight. That seemed like a sad awakening to a bright
dream. We did enjoy the day so much, May and I, but
just think that I never got the letter about Papa's coming
till he had gone.

"Of course I feel somewhat lonely now, but then I'm

going home in so short a time, and Papa says he will make an effort to go back this way at the same time I do ; won't that be charming !

"Now I must thank you for the present you sent me. It is *so* nice, and I wanted just such a one very much, but could not get time to make it.

"I have nearly one hundred flowers analysed, but that is only half the number required. Miss S. has advised us to give up botany this series and finish it next year, as she thinks it would be far better for us to get the autumn flowers, so I have taken her advice, and have Physiology instead. The new series commences to-day.

"Love to all, and thank mamma for her letter. I will answer it as soon as possible.

"Yours Lovingly,

"ANNIE."

—————

"JUNE 8th, 1868.

"OWN SISTER,

"I have a little minute to spare and will devote it to you, for I think you are a ready and patient listener.

"I meant to say that I have left my botany till next *summer* term, instead of fall, so your inference is unfounded. As to Hamilton, I've left the subject for the present, as there is no need of immediate decision, but I hope to be directed about my path ; if I should go there simply to please myself, I am too enlightened to expect success or satisfaction. I want a willingness to be guided entirely by Providence, and I know that you will all make it a subject of prayer. Though papa scarcely mentioned the subject, yet I think he inclines to the idea that I had better stay here. What do you think about continuing your course at school? A great many have enquired lately if you were not coming back here.

"At last Thursday evening meeting we were addressed by Mr. Harper of Canton, China, a missionary. He gave us some very interesting intelligence about the moral and intellectual condition of China, though his manner of speaking was very monotonous. China proper extends over a territory equal to that occupied by the United States, exclusive of the territories. The system of education seems very thorough, no one being allowed to hold any public office who has not taken a degree, while the education of the women is no less carefully attended to. Most of the trustees were here on Thursday and had a grand 'trustee meeting' in the north wing parlor; they were consulting on the best means of disposing of *our forty thousand.* Mrs. Durant has promised to give five thousand dollars' worth of books, if a new building be erected specially for a library; so 'we' are going to secure her generous donation by fulfilling the conditions.

---

"Tuesday Morning.

"May and I expect to go to Amherst this evening. It is 'class day' for the college there, and the public exercises will probably be very interesting, so Alice is to bring a carriage for us this afternoon and we will stay till to-morrow night, *if we can get permission.*

"I suppose you heard about the ceremonies throughout the State last month, when the graves of the union soldiers were strewn with flowers. It was observed here, and our *brass drum* and *fife* paraded before the long procession, playing 'Nellie Gray' with very rapid movement.

"I must thank mamma for her precious little letter; it was delightful, mamma.

"You mentioned in one of your letters having obtained Tasso's 'Jerusalem Delivered;' are you reading it in Italian? I have been reading it lately, but the translations probably take much from its beauty. I think it never has been very well translated, but I may be mistaken in this.

"Well darlings, good night,

"ANNIE."

———

"Room 100, June 13, 1868.

"SISTER MINE,

"This lovely summer day, arrayed in a fresh buff calico, and enjoying the balmy air from my open window, I would fain share my enjoyment (especially the buff calico!) with some whom I long to see; this being impossible, I will hold a little pen and ink conversation with you. The conviction creeps upon me that we may yet have a little summer in spite of the discouraging signs and predictions. This sunny day proves somebody a false prophet.

"Do you want to hear the Seminary news? The senior

class have elected their officers, and they are as follows :
C. M., President ; R. K. and J. B., Vice-Presidents ; M. D.,
Treasurer ; N. E., Secretary ; A. F., M. B., L. C. and A. C.,
Prophetesses ; and L. M. and C. P., Poetesses. This arrangement seems to be quite satisfactory to all parties,
and I am sure C. is the best one they could have chosen
for President.

"Item number two—we have had a missionary here.
Strange event ! Mr. Douglass, from India, spoke to us
yesterday, instead of the usual hall exercise. He is a fine
looking man, and his account was the most interesting I
have heard for a long time. His mission is to the
*Tullugoos* (at least so pronounced), and he first mentioned
the impression any one would receive on entering one of
the large cities. The streets are broad and neat; the
houses large and handsome, while the mercantile estab-
lishments furnish every article of commerce, and in some
the number of clerks varies from twenty to thirty.
Observing the industrious habits of the people, their fine
personal appearance and general intelligence, as well as
theirenquiring minds and power of intellect, ' every prospect pleases,' and it is only by obtaining an insight into
their false and degrading system of religion, that the dark
side of the picture is seen, and the discovery made that
truly 'man is vile.'

"The state of woman in India may be known from the
fact that she is supposed to have no *soul*. As we know,
the system of *caste* is the greatest barrier to the progress
of the Gospel, but on this the effect of British rule is

plainly seen. There are now railways traversing the country in many directions, and 'every time the old engine leaves the station it dashes over the steel network of caste, which is shutting out the people from all hope of rise and progress, and *crushes it to pieces.*' You are aware that those belonging to one grade or caste consider themselves polluted by even sitting in the same room with those of another, but, in order to take advantage of the rapid railway travelling, they must do this; and here we see how powerful is the love of gain, for, rather than spend the much greater amount of time and money required by the old means of travelling they constantly pollute themselves by this means, though they endeavor to counteract the effect of this by more numerous ablutions. It seems evident that these modern improvements must be instrumental, in time, in working a wonderful revolution.

"Mr. Douglass related to us some conversations he had had with the Brahmins, assuring us that it was no fancy sketch, but that he was simply giving us a sample of the questionings they were constantly called upon to answer. In their questions they commenced with God's eternal existence and brought out clearly the fact that the whole creation as we find it now is the result of a pre-conceived plan in the Divine mind; then going back over the train of argument, step by step, traced back to God the origin of sin, calling upon Mr. Douglass to acknowledge that this was the inevitable result of his teaching. He readily showed them that they had made a fatal mistake by basing their argument on the supposition that this Creator was an unholy being, and so on.

"His object in telling us this was to let us see, what are some of the obstacles they have to contend with in the subtle reasoning they are called upon to answer, and the extensive cultivation of those minds yet in the darkness of heathenism.

"Altogether I got quite a different idea of India from Mr. Douglass, than from the numerous other missionaries who have talked to us about it.

"Do you think that is sufficient for India?

"I must say a word now to darling mamma.

"Yours, pet,

"ANNIE."

———

"June 19th, 1868.

"On Wednesday morning A. H. and I walked down to Smith's Ferry and took the cars for Northampton.

"A. had some shopping to do, so we walked up and down 'Shop Row' till it was time for the train to start—about half-past ten. We started back for South Hadley, walking to the ferry again.

"It was a very warm day, but we contemplated a journey up Mount Tom in the afternoon, so resolved not to feel tired. Instead of going down to dinner I took a refreshing bath, and laid down for a short time, and felt quite rested when it was time to get ready. The Natural History Society were going on an excursion, first down the Connecticut to examine the bird tracks, and then up Mount Tom.

"We all wore gymnastic suits, and found them most comfortable. The party consisted of about thirty, including six teachers.

"Miss F. and Miss C. rode almost all the way up the mountain, while the rest of us walked. How I wished you were with us to enjoy the ascent. I should like to go up every week. Miss F. found out that A., H., and I had walked to and from the ferry in the morning, and almost insisted on having us ride, but we would not, as that would have spoiled half the enjoyment; then Miss F. said, playfully, she supposed we were preparing to be excused from exercises for the next few days; but how different the result.

"When the day was over we were not as tired as when it commenced, and I have felt better ever since; though, to be sure, my face is several shades darker, and finely variegated with freckles.

"Oh! this Connecticut Valley is truly beautiful! But I have not time to expatiate. The bell summons me away.

"Good morning pet, and love to all."

(The following letter alludes to plans for visiting her brother during vacation.)

———

"June 29th, 1868.

"M. DEAREST,

"I am very sorry mamma has changed her plans, but suppose it must be for the best. It would have been such a pleasure to T. to see mamma, and of course much pleasanter for me not to go alone, but I ought to be perfectly satisfied if papa allows me to go at all.

"However, M., you must not think of my being 'tardy in returning,' nor must I allow myself to contemplate such a thing. I *must* graduate in '70, if nothing but my own ability is in the way. Just think, I have a double delight in view; going to see T., and going home. I must not stay in New York long, for my vacation will be *so* short. I know you will all pray that my visit to T. may not be without profit to both of us. I feel quite anxious lest it should be otherwise.

"Our Natural History Society holds its annual meeting in the parlors this evening, for the purpose of electing officers, and having a pleasant time generally.

"Miss S. hinted to me quite plainly that any flowers peculiar to the Canadian flora, would be gratefully received, and I mean to try and enrich the society's herbarium a little if I can.

"You ask about our recess meetings; they are very interesting, at least as much so as last year, and Miss B. is anxious that they should be profitable; but this closing term has so much in it to dissipate our minds, that there is no unusual interest in the school. The monthly concerts are interesting as ever. We had lately a beautiful letter from Mrs. 'Katy Lloyd,' a very long one, which I would like to copy if I could obtain possession of it, for I am sure you would be exceedingly interested in it. You know what a noble woman she is, and how thrillingly she writes of her work in that heathen land.

"Our poor cherry trees are all blighted, and we cannot regale ourselves on them, as we were wont to do of old.

"Mr. Foote, of Howard Mission, is intending to visit Canada in the summer, with some of his *little ones*, and probably the B. girls will accompany the party; if so, they are pretty confident of visiting Ottawa, which will be quite pleasant for us 'Holyoke girls,' will it not?

"Mr. Jenkins, Congregational minister from Amherst preached to us on Sunday; in the morning on the subject of 'Graces before Gifts,' as being the Bible order. His language is simple and his manner unaffected; yet there is great beauty and force in his expression of ideas, and I have seldom listened to anyone with such satisfaction. He contrasted the spirit of the world, and especially of the American nation, in esteeming and assiduously cultivating talent, shrewdness, and business capacity, with that of the Bible, which places far above everything else, the attainment of charity, including all the graces.

"A still more beautiful discourse in the afternoon was on the office of Christ as our *King*; a character in which He is so seldom distinctly represented to us.

"You must read 'De Senectute' when I go home; it is very interesting, and some of Mr. Cicero's ideas are quite charming, but Cato, whom he represents as the author, is terribly egotistical.

"My letter has quite lengthened out after all, and I've been such a short time scribbling it, but my fingers are aching with the unnatural speed at which my pen flies.

"Love to all, pet one, from

"Your Sister, and

"Mamma's Daughter,

"ANNIE."

"July 4th, 1868.

"DEAR M.,

"On this the morning of our *glorious* 'fourth,' I snatch a moment from the busy turmoil to give you some idea of the present state of affairs.

"In the first place, this is a holiday, and the Senior's class day, and altogether we are having a very exciting time, so much so that I can hardly guide my pen. Some idea of the cause of the excitement may be gleaned from the toast given for the teachers last night at the class supper; it was thus :—

"' There is a Destiny that shapes our ends *rough*; hew them as we will.' Please note the new style of punctuation, else you will not see the point. * * I got to sleep about twelve o'clock, and slept, with the exception of several waking intervals, till finally wakened by the dinging of the church bells and booming of cannon, this morning very early.

"We did not get up till nearly time for the *five*, and then were called to the front balcony to witness the exhibition of the 'Calathumpians' ('Fantastics' or 'Horribles' as they are called here), and with streaming hair, and most imperfect toilets we hastened out. It was very comical.

"Last night they had a cake containing a ring and a thimble; May got the thimble and F. C. the ring, the thimble signifying the old maid of the class, and the ring the class bride. This morning the Seniors are having a meeting in the lecture room, and so May dressed up in the most old maidish manner possible, with hair combed over her face and terminating in a little pug at the top of her head, all surmounted by a mammoth comb, meekly folded handkerchief round her neck, huge check apron, and a pepper box supposed to contain snuff, at her waist, in company with a pair of scissors, work box and huge · palmleaf fan; while she squinted her eyes through a pair of gold bowed spectacles. F. C. was dressed as a bride, with a white dress and flowing white veil fastened with flowers. D. N. dressed up to represent the bridegroom, in knickerbockers and black velvet tunic, with her short curly hair parted at the side. I never saw her look so pretty. They were heartily cheered as they entered the lecture room; but Miss E. expressed her disapproval.

"The sun shines gloriously on the stars and stripes gently waving before my eyes, and almost I feel as if I had an interest in the general rejoicing. Do any but Holyoke girls get excited over such little things?

"The weather is pleasantly cool to-day; it was oppressively warm yesterday, ninety-three in the shade, one hundred and six in the sun. May and I were sitting in our room in the morning, dressed in the lightest manner possible, when Miss S. passed by our door and looked in to ask us if we did not wish with somebody—(I forget who) that we could 'take off our flesh and sit in our bones.' Miss S. is so humorous and pleasant, everyone likes her very much.

"We had a dusky-browed Japanese to hear us sing this afternoon. He is attending college in Monson, near here,

with three more of his countrymen.  He is strange looking, no whiskers and long straight black hair, and not a
very animated countenance.

"To-morrow is the last study day before reviews, and
then how rapidly the time will go.

" Love to all the loved ones, from

" Your loving

. " ANNIE."

---

" JULY 9th, 1868.

" By the way, I never told you about the paper
mill, did I ?  Perhaps I have time now, but then I never
can describe such things respectably.

" We took our umbrellas, for it threatened rain when
we started, but when we drove up to the long brick building with its innumerable windows, the sun was shining
gloriously, and we walked round first to get a good view
of the Falls which had power to shake our Seminary, and
whose roar occasionally aspired to reach South Hadley
cars.  It was a fine sight, but you have a finer in our
beautiful Chaudière, on which you can feast undisturbed
by the ceaseless clash of machinery.

"Intimating our desire to watch the process of
paper-making, to a little man in the doorway, we were
conducted to a large room, roughly finished, where some
twenty or thirty girls were busily engaged in sorting the
rags, and cutting them up on a knife resembling half a
sword blade, which was fixed to the stand of each one.
The girls were intelligent looking, as most Yankee girls

are. They had to wear something over their heads to protect them from the dust and lint, and it was amusing to see the variety of tastes displayed in the arrangement of this head dress. Some of the more sedate had simply a large handkerchief plainly folded round the forehead, while others, with more pretensions to beauty, had arranged theirs in a turban shape, decorated with soiled rosettes and goose feathers.

"We went from this room to another where some large boxes of snowy white pulp were standing, and where were large wooden receptacles, some twelve or fifteen feet long, of an oval shape, in which masses of pulp and water were slowly revolving. (You can get an idea of how it looked by taking a piece of blue paper and *masticating* it well.) We could not see the machinery, but saw that a change was effected which made the mass smoother; from this room it was carried to the final process. It was first passed on to a series of flat receivers, something like sieves, which allowed the water to ooze slowly through them, leaving the pulp which grew drier and drier as it passed over each successive sieve; these were all heated to aid in the process, which was all carried on by quite simple machinery. It gradually became paper like, and when it is about as firm as wet blotting paper, it is carried over rollers resting on flannel to prevent it from tearing. These rollers are heated, and when the paper arrives at the last one it is in firm white sheets, about the width of wall paper, and is cut by a machine at the end.

"The next room was large, airy and clean, and here also a great many women and girls were employed, some in counting and others in folding the clean white paper; so clean, that no one would have suspected its close relationship to the uninviting rags we had first beheld.

"Now dear, you probably know *almost* as much about the process as you did before I commenced.

\*　　\*　　\*　　\*　　\*　　\*

"The more I study, the more I see the absurdity of calling that *education*, which is simply storing the mind with facts, or making it the object of study to convert the mind into a crowded encyclopedia. If this were all our aim, think how unsatisfactory it would be, after years of patient study, to compare our mite of knowledge with the untold amount of which we are yet strangers.

"I am very anxious to read Gibbon's 'Decline and Fall of the Roman Empire;' Willson, author of our Ancient History, quotes from him freely, and it was my delight to commit to memory some of these beautiful passages. We must have it sometime, or try and find a more interesting history than 'Rollin's Ancient.' Perhaps, however, we did not give that a fair trial.

"So, like a little witch, you want to make me 'stay out' again, do you? You would not surely have me give up graduating in '70. I could not venture to stay away the first of the year at any rate; if I find it possible may in the latter part of it.

"How delightful it was to get *four* letters from home

in *three* days.   Well, my enthusiastic little Italian, I must say good night, and imagine I hear you say, 'it's time.'

" May every blessing rest upon my loved home.

" Yours, darling,

"ANNIE G. J."

---

" July 20, 1868.

" MON CHER PERE,

" Your letter was a real feast.   I knew it would be when you did write; and I shall be so glad of the Ottawa papers.

" I believe I tried in my last letter to explain to M. the cause of the President's impeachment, but I wrote in a hurry, and really do not know how fully I explained it.

" The President's cabinet is composed of the Secretaries of War, Navy, State, Treasury, Interior and Post-office Departments.   These are all appointed by the President, *by and with the advice and consent of the Senate.*

" Almost all the Articles of Impeachment (which are eleven) are based on the President's violation of the Tenure of Office Bill, passed by last Congress.   This has been considered a part of the Constitution, though I believe a question as to its validity has been raised, and not yet decided by the courts.   The President in his defence sometimes claims that it is not valid and that, therefore, he had a perfect right to remove Stanton (the sole power of removal being previously vested in the President); and again, he says, he did it to *test* the validity of the Bill. He also argues that, as Stanton was not appointed by him, but by President Lincoln, the clause in that Bill providing that secretaries shall hold their offices during the term of the President by whom they have been appointed, does not apply to him. The President has no power to appoint any one to, or remove him from, office during a session of the Senate, except with its advice and consent. If he removes an officer and appoints a successor during a recess of the Senate he must, at its next Session, apprise the Senate of this and give his reasons, and if they concur the appointment is confirmed; if not, the one suspended returns to his office. Now you will see that at the close of the Session, the President could again make what appointment he chose, as he did when he first removed Stanton, but the Tenure of Office Bill prevents this by providing that if no appointment is made during the Session, with its advice and consent, the office remains in abeyance, and the duties are performed by some other member of the Department.

"If any one accepts any such office to which he has been thus unconstitutionally appointed, he is liable to a fine not exceeding $10,000, or imprisonment not exceeding five years, by the same comprehensive Bill. This is the ground on which General Thomas has been arrested. I do not know that this will be very intelligible, but I think it is correct. * * * * * *

"My recitations come now at the third and fourth recitation hours in the morning, so that I have the whole afternoon for study, but I do not like it much.

"I am apt to spend too much time over my botany, in

which I delight. My room is perfumed now with the beautiful wild Azalea. A. H. gives me all the botanical 'specimens' she finds, which is quite an assistance.

"I do want mamma to come to South Hadley and see all the beauties of nature surrounding it. Both mamma and you will of *course* come to see me graduate; but that is piercing the future rather too far.

"We Middlers had a 'class meeting' in room G on Saturday. We met to make arrangements for trimming the Sem. Hall, as that duty always devolves on the middle class. I am one of the committee on ferns and have to go off hunting for them at the rising bell to-morrow morning. We are to have a large hanging basket in the centre of the hall with hemlock wreaths festooned from the posts. The class motto of '66 is to be put up over the clock, and the rest of the room is to be ornamented with brackets and bouquets.

"The house is full of 'former graduates' and it is a bustling, but withal a pleasant time.

"Yours most lovingly,
"ANNIE G. JOHNSON."

## V.

### 1868-1869.

Another long happy summer vacation passed all too quickly in the loved home, and the dear one returned to commence her senior middle year at the Seminary.

It was a great trial for the fond parents and sisters to part with her in this way, year after year, but all looked forward to the happy period, when, her studies completed, she should return to be the loved and trusted companion of her father, mother and brothers, and the guide of her younger sisters.

Her mother and sister M. accompanied her as far as Ogdensburg, from which place they returned home, leaving her to continue her journey alone. The ensuing letter details her experiences until her arrival at the village in which the brother resided with whom she was to pass a few days before returning to the Seminary. Allusion has been made in former letters to this projected visit.

" WISCOY, Sept. 12, 1868.

"DARLING ONES,

"Mamma and M. will remember they left me sitting in the ominbus at the railway station, at Ogdensburg. From that point I returned to the Seymour House.

paid our bill, and was carried off to the Rome and Water-town depôt.

"The ride to Rome was pleasant, though in the evening the cars became very much crowded. A gentleman who shared my seat, kindly obtained all necessary information about my stay and change of cars at Rome.

"Before eleven I was on my way to Rochester, by the New York Central route. Being resolved to sleep, if possible, I got 'scrooged up' (thanks to M. for coining so apropos a term), on a seat, and enjoyed a tolerably comfortable slumber till wakened by our arrival at Syracuse. My shawl, though not absolutely necessary as a protection, did good service as a pillow. An uneventful ride of three hours more brought me to Rochester. Here I got out, found my trunks, but waited in vain for the conflicting calls of 'Clinton Hotel,' 'Osborne House' and many another house. A most unwelcome stillness and order prevailed, and mentally running over E's direction, 'arrived at Rochester, take cab for Clinton Hotel,' I anxiously enquired of a lazy looking official where a cab or omnibus was to be found. Imagine my dismay when told that there would be none there till seven in the morning, at the earliest. The station was uninviting. I must go to the Clinton Hotel to see if T. was there and to get my breakfast (for I was *so* hungry), and get to the Valley depôt before half-past seven. The situation was perplexing, but I resolved to make the best of it. It was just half-past three, and I was almost overcome with sleepiness, but the awkward division of the seats by iron *arms* precluded the possibility of even reclining. Between my sleepy nods I noticed a small boy roll head first off a seat and sprawl on the floor, where he continued to lie, evidently undisturbed by its soiled condition. A large table before me was occupied by two slumbering youths. On the opposite side of the room some benevolent individual had removed an arm, making a comfortable lounge where a maiden reclined for some time; she, however, took her departure before long, when I speedily secured her place. After a somewhat disturbed sleep, I awoke and found it near six o'clock. After a hasty ablution and arrangement of my hair, I went out to watch for a cab, but evidently Rochester was not an early riser. On enquiry I learned it was but fifteen minutes walk to the Clinton Hotel, and resolved to find it for myself; this I did without much difficulty, but found that T. had not been there. I had my name registered and enquired for breakfast, which was provided for me in a little private dining-room. On the advice of *the man* at the Clinton House, I went back to the same depôt instead of the one to which E. directed me, and took the seven-twenty train to Portage, changed cars at Batavia and Attica, but the travelling was slow, and after we left Attica the engine broke down completely, and we were detained for an hour or so. We dragged along and reached Portage station at last, where the stage was ready to start for the village. At a quarter past twelve I greeted the fat landlord in Portage; still no sign of T. The stage for Wiscoy not having come, I sat down to wait. Time

J

passed, but no stage did I see, though receiving frequent assurance that 'it would be here directly.' After a weary two hours a girl informed me that the 'gentleman' who drove the stage was just eating his dinner, and would start at its conclusion. As time passed my inward comments upon the 'gentleman's' appetite grew less and less flattering, but I have reason to believe that his inner man was satisfied at last, for the stage made its appearance at the door before three o'clock. On the way the driver coolly informed me that he could take me within a mile of Mrs. D's., but no farther. I laughingly enquired what he supposed I was going to do then; well, he thought I'd 'have to take my chance for a team.' Hoping for the best, we drove on till we came to my driver's destination. Standing by the 'store' was a small one-seated wagon with no vestige of a place for a trunk; hence, I was somewhat unbelieving when the driver ejaculated 'there's your chance.' However, seeing my trunk thrust into the shabby little vehicle, I prepared to follow, trusting to find a spot for my feet *outside*, if not in the wagon. Where my driver was to sit was an unexplained mystery, and my perplexity was no way diminished when I saw a huge bag poised on top of my trunk; but I soon found how greatly I had underrated his power of adaptation to circumstances, for directly he was nicely balanced on the edge of the seat with his feet gracefully dangling over the wheel. A mail-bag was next attached to the end of a rein for safe keeping, but I thought the climax was reached when among the promiscuous assemblage was thrust a twelve-foot bundle of walnut trimmings. Though trembling for the living freight on board, I hoped we were ready to start, when from behind us came the anxious enquiry, ' where are you going to put me?' I turned round to see the puzzled face of an old man who had come in the same stage with me. After seeing *him* accommodated I should scarcely have been surprised to hear them offering the horse a seat among us. Somewhat to the surprise of the driver, I here indulged in a hearty laugh at the novelty of my situation. The old man, whom I have learned is an Austrian, was inclined to be sociable, and he soon discovered that I was a Canadian, and ' the minister's' sister." * *

————

" Monday Morning.

" T. and I are just starting off for a drive, and this letter must go to the office, but I will continue it this evening and tell the rest.

" Of course I found T., met him at the post office, but he had not received either of our letters.

" Yours lovingly,

" ANNIE."

————

" September 22nd, 1868.

" DARLING M.,

" Our first Tuesday evening ! How I would love to be home !

" I have waited and waited for a chance to tell you

about what I saw at Portage, and now feel rather too hurried, but will try and tell you something.

"The road from Wiscoy to Portage is very beautiful, as I remarked, greatly to the surprise of the 'natives.' The Genesee flows through a pleasant valley, while on either side of it stretch away beautiful richly wooded hills. I was constantly surprised with scraps of the most exquisite scenery ; a shallow stream, with a pebbly, sunlit beach on one side, and a green bank, willow-fringed, throwing its shadow on the other, while above and around were the fresh green hills, and the calm blue sky.

"At the village of Portage the canal crosses the river on a high bridge, supported by some massive stone-work. Pretty little waterfalls are now trickling through and falling musically into the rocky bed of the stream beneath. After crossing the bridge the canal winds round the hill-side at a considerable height above the river, and here there is little appearance of art to mar its beauty. Just here, also, the famous bridge adds interest to the scene.

" After leaving this spot there was little variety in the road till we swept round a curve and found ourselves at the beautiful ivy-covered gate which forms the entrance to ' Glen Iris.'

" Leaving our horse outside we went up the neat gravel walk, admiring as we went the tasteful arrangement of a creeping convolvolus, or a tiny bed of brilliant flowers. At some distance from the gate stood the house ; a rather plain structure, but transformed and beautified by a profusion of the most luxuriant vines.

"Turning to the right we found a miniature lake with a fountain in the centre, and at the foot of a tiny stone pier a little rowboat.

"All around the trees presented a lovely combination of colours, and close to the water's edge the vines crept and twined themselves with a most bewitching grace.

"The retiring bell! And I've not yet come to the rustic seat where one might sit for days and gaze on the wealth of beauty lavished on all around. The foaming, snowy waterfall, dashing gaily over the great immovable rock, on which, in dark, cool shade, bits of moss creep out, and to whose rough sides dripping vines cling tenderly; while down the great ravine dances the bright little stream, all unawed by the frowning rocks which tower majestically above it.

"Yes, M. dear, I must bid you a reluctant good night, hoping to resume this fascinating theme when I can get more time. *If I only could* tell you how beautiful that spot is—but it is only spoiling it for me to attempt to give you any description.

"Thanks to pet A. for her letter; will answer it soon. Love to E. and all.

"Yours, darling,<br>"ANNIE."

———

"Oct. 13, 1868.

"DARLING SISTER M.,

"Your dear little letter containing my brooch came this evening; how acceptable it was, you yourself can judge.

"I do enjoy my philosophy very much indeed. It is delightful, and though twenty-five pages is no short lesson, I find it easier than my history. Miss S. is our teacher.

"Our reading lessons are very interesting, and if we follow them up by faithful and persevering practice, will prove a great benefit I have no doubt. In speaking of pronunciation Prof. Churchill told us that English people had a right to demand that Americans should pronounce the English language as it is pronounced in the best London circles; just as a Frenchman would wish us to follow the Parisian standard in speaking French. He spoke of the fact that English ladies are distinguished by the elegance and correctness of their language, and their clear enunciation. The Queen has paid great attention to this, and in her parliamentary speeches not a syllable of what she says is lost, though she preserves an ordinary tone of voice. What must decide the pronunciation of words is 'the general usage in the best London circles,' and this is the guide followed by Worcester and Webster, as well as other *dictionary writers*.

"The Professor advises us to study the dictionary, recommending for our use 'Webster's new, unabridged.'"

"Our pronunciation of *wound* is correct, as also many other words which disagree with the prevailing pronunciation here."

———

"Wednesday evening.

"A dull day, varied only by a lecture. After lecture, which was at four o'clock, F. and I went out for a walk;

we met K. P., a pretty little foreigner, and she accompanied us ; afterwards M. R. and her room-mate came up
with us, and we all started to go round Prospect Hill
' the square ' you know. We raced and tumbled along
in a most undignified manner, considering that there was
a senior and a senior middler in the party.

" Miss B. is still my section teacher. She is very sweet,
and has our recess meetings in her own room; they are
dear little meetings. I have been trying to overcome my
exclusive habits and see more of the girls, but it is hard
work.

" With love to all, and wishing you every good blessing,

"  I am, your own loving sister,

" ANNIE."

" P. S. Come home next vacation ? Nay ! *Don't expect it.*"

———

" Nov. 1st, 1868.

" DARLING SISTER M.

" Having given your letter a second perusal, I sit
down with a most *satisfactory impression* to commence
a letter in return.

" I've been quite remiss in my correspondence this term
I fear, but my studies demand my time so imperatively
that I have had to give myself up to them almost entirely.

" Let me see : in my last letter I told you about Col.
Baylor's visit—in this one I hope to report the sayings

and doings of Gen. Howard, who is expected to spend Sunday with us—to-morrow. He is a member of the Freedman's Bureau, and a very active, devoted Christian.

"Prof. Churchill has returned, and into the midst of our multitudinous duties is crowded a daily lecture; but then they are enjoyable, and I think very instructive, if only we don't forget them as soon as he goes.

"'I think if you don't go to C. M's that you'll come home.' A calm little sentence but full of a quiet certainty; a suggestive sentence; the grave doubts that hung about my fate for the vacation are being dispelled; but by what course of consultation and argument I am not told. A self-willed little sentence; however cherished and pleasant the plans *I* may have formed, they are not to stand for a moment against that determined 'you'll come home.'

"Well, little diplomat, I stand ready to accept the mandate, whatever it may be, and you know as well as I, whither my most eager inclinations turn.

"No, M., I'm not very lonely without a room-mate. It was with a feeling of almost desparing homesickness that I came to my deserted room after F. went away, but the comfort I take in my solitude now, is a *striking* illustration of our wonderful power of adaptation to circumstances.

"Many thanks for the papers. They contained a great many items of interest to me. I can gather more English news from our papers, than from those we have here. My increasing knowledge of the past history of Europe, makes its present history much more interesting to me."

" Sunday morning.

" The elements are waging fierce warfare this morning. The rain pours down in torrents, and the weeping willow opposite my window wildly flings its arms about in an agony of supplication to the merciless wind. We are all excused from attendance at church, but then I must go to hear Gen. Howard. Mr. Smith, a minister from New York, led devotions, and gave us a very earnest and rather beautiful address.

" This will be a busy day, for our Bible lesson requires long study. We are commencing the first book of Kings, and glancing at our topics I see that they require a knowledge of Profane as well as Sacred History. We cannot get time to do our Bible lessons justice, for our topics are never given us till Sunday morning.

" Later.—Instead of having service in the church, the town's people came into the Seminary, so that we all had the privilege of attending without facing the uncomfortable storm.

" Mr. Green opened the service, and made a few remarks in which he spoke of the mistake so many make, in thinking that diligence in business is incompatible with an earnest, faithful service of Christ; giving, as an example of the contrary, the busy, toilsome life of Gen. Howard, and his constant devotion to the work of God.

" Mr. Smith, who is the field agent of the American Missionary Society, then rose and talked to us about the work among the Freedmen. He first described the field of labor, showing how ready the negroes are to receive the truth and yield themselves to the influences of the Gospel. Unlike the foreign missionary, the laborer here has but little opposition to contend with : no deeply rooted prejudices, and none of the unnatural, acquired reserve which characterizes the youth of the north. A rich harvest awaits every willing laborer. On the other hand, the work demands a great sacrifice of any one who engages in it. There is an almost complete isolation from society, and as the northern teacher is looked upon with contempt by all the whites of any standing, he, or she, has to endure a species of social ostracism. One young lady, after teaching in a certain town for ten years, said, that in all that time she had not spoken to a single white person save the clerk of the post-office who delivered her letters. How galling it must be to endure scorn and contempt from inferiors in everything but wealth or social standing. Mr. Smith continued to speak in a most interesting manner for about half an hour, and then Gen. Howard, ' the hero of a hundred battles,' rose, the empty sleeve by his side adding to the interest with which we looked upon him. He is rather fine looking, heavily built, with iron-gray hair, and dark whiskers. His voice is powerful, though not sweet, and he has a slightly English accent, reminding me occasionally of Lord C., though his pronunciation is not the same.

" He spoke of the curse slavery had been to the land ; a constant reproach to them as a people boasting of free institutions. Also of the predictions and fears that a sudden, complete emancipation would be followed by great distress and anarchy. That these predictions may not be fulfilled it is necessary for the people of the North to undertake the work of Christianizing and civilising these ignorant millions with earnestness and determination. Then followed an earnest appeal to all of us, to consecrate ourselves, not to this or any particular work now, but to be ready for any work to which the Master may call us. An unconverted woman, said he, is not fit for any position in life. He closed his address with a persuasive invitation to the unconverted ones, to come to Jesus.

" Perhaps, dear, you are almost weary of this talk ; but we are apt to write about what interests us most at the time, and I have indulged my inclination.

" I am half afraid to go home for fear something may happen to make me tardy in returning. I feel that that must not occur again, if it is possible to avoid it. My natural love of approbation makes me shrink from the danger of earning a character for want of promptness and punctuality—though I think that hitherto my delinquency has been unavoidable.

" Love to all at home, dear.

" Your

" A. G. J."

————

" November 3rd, 1868.

" M. DARLING,

" Grant or Seymour ! Which is it ?

" This is the burden of our song. To-morrow we shall know the result of to-day's momentous elections. Defeat

or victory !  Twice have I had the pleasure of giving in
my vote for Grant without having to undergo the tedious
process of naturalization.

"Miss F. sent two girls round yesterday to take a vote
of the school, and out of two hundred and seventy votes
recorded, two hundred and sixty-two were for Grant and
*eight* for Seymour.  We are emphatically a Republican
school.

"Perhaps you think it absurd for me to manifest such
a lively interest in what is not supposed to concern me at
all, but who could read the papers we have before us and
remain neutral ?

"If the result is what we almost all wish, we shall
probably have an illumination to-morrow evening.

"By the way, dear papa, can you send me a few papers
containing English news ?  I do not quite understand,
and cannot ascertain here, the exact position of the English government at present, or the change that has taken
place on account of the recent Reform Bill.  I should be
so glad to see any *English* papers you have.  Do you
never have the London *Times ?*  Miss F. said she was
very anxious to have it in our reading room.

Nov. 9, 1868.

"Well, M., Grant is elected ! (new and startling intelligence to you doubtless).  We had our illumination ;
sang America, Star-spangled Banner, Yankee Doodle, and
other patriotic airs.  The *Springfield Republican,* and
*Boston Journal* make honorable mention of our enthus-

iastic demonstration, not even forgetting the cheering (which I think it's well for Mr. Grant's peace of mind that he did not hear). But that impertinent little ' Amherst Student' ungallantly remarks, ' Each young lady put her lamp in the window, and then went out to look at it and cheer it.'

" Gen. Howard is an intimate friend of Gen. Grant, and was constantly brought into contact with him during the war. In conversation here, he described Mr. Grant as a man who has a very strong trust in Providence ; he is quite incapable of the least profanity, and seems to have a profound reverence for God. At one time he was asked why he did not seek a certain promotion which it was likely he might obtain—his answer was, ' I should be afraid to do it, lest I might be flying in the face of Providence.'

" This is encouraging for the nation."

―――――

"Nov. 16th, 1868.

"MINNIE DARLING,

"School closes just one week from to-morrow night, on the twenty-fourth of this month, a fact of which I have thought so little that it greatly astonished me this evening. Four or five other girls are going to board at Mrs. W's in Amherst, so I will not want for company.

" Prof. Churchill has gone at last. On Friday evening he gave us a reading in the Sem. Hall ; some of the ' town' came in, and we had some good music. The professor read two selections from Jean Ingelow, one, the old sailor's prayer in 'Brothers, and a Sermon,' the other, 'High tide on the Coast of Lincolnshire'; you remember it :—

> " Sweeter woman ne'er drew breath,
> Than my son's wife, Elizabeth," etc.

" It was such a satisfaction to hear these my favorite poems, read so beautifully.

" Oh, that you could have heard and seen him read Shakspeare. He read a scene from Hamlet; the conversation of the two grave-diggers and Hamlet, ending with Hamlet's apostrophe to the skull of 'poor Yorick'; you can get your book now and read it, but you will not *see* it all, as he made us see it. I became so excited over it that it gave me an idea of how fascinated I would be with the theatre.

" This was followed by some selections from Dickens; an irresistibly comical dialogue from Pickwick Papers, and that affecting scene in Oliver Twist where the pompous 'parochial beadle,' Mr. Bumble, and the matron of the parochial poor-house, Mrs. Corney, conclude to join hearts and house-keeping.

" Last selection was a piece describing the taking of a subscription in a Roman Catholic church, by a priest, 'Father Phil's Collection.' It almost threw us into convulsions, and yet there were such real merit and beauty in it, that it induced smiles and tears by turns.

" Such a performance was worth a dozen elocution lessons.

" Don't forget to send me the 'Farmer's Mass' in B flat, M.; we commence singing it to-morrow evening."

"Tuesday Evening.

"Behold the uncertainty of all a school-girl's plans! Yesterday I wrote to A. W., accepting her invitation, to-day I am again a waif, as far as vacation is concerned. Just after putting my letter in the letter-box this morning, I heard a rumour that no girls were to be allowed to board in Amherst. Later in the morning Miss F. came up to see if my room was warm, and I mentioned this rumour to her, at the same time stating that I had made my plans for vacation. Miss F. confirmed the report, and went on to explain why she did not think it best for us to go to Amherst. Of course the chief objection is the fact of the college being there, and though this cannot apply to me personally, yet there certainly are some who cannot be trusted to conduct themselves properly in the vicinity of such a bugbear. I cannot reasonably expect her to make an exception in my favor, and submit with the best grace possible. However, she did not really forbid my going, but only *advised* me kindly. On my telling her that I expected to go as a guest, she said she would advise me to go and pay a visit of a day or too, but not longer.

"My cheerful acquiescence in this overturning of my plans, instead of expressing indignation at the infringement of my rights as a young lady of discretion, must be attributed to mamma. That little talk of hers on the subject of 'love of approbation,' set me thinking, and the result of my thinking was the conviction that I have been altogether too independent of the opinion of others, and too positive of my own ability to judge for myself of the propriety of anything I wished to undertake.

"We sang for the first time this evening. Oh! that Mass is beautiful! I noticed in the *Times* some weeks ago, a suggestion about forming a society for the practice of some of the standard music, and I inwardly hoped the affair would be put into practice. Ottawa is so far behind American cities in this respect.

"One week from to-night I'll feel free, and pretty happy, if I *am* still in the Seminary. Perhaps I will go to Northampton, Granby, or Monson, and then for a day or two at the last to Amherst.

" Yours lovingly,

" ANNIE G. JOHNSON."

———

" Nov. 19th, 1868.

"DEAREST PAPA,

" Your account of the affairs in England was very interesting, though not all new to me. The papers here give such a very meagre outline of what is going on that they are quite unsatisfactory, and I thought perhaps some of our papers would have speeches in them, or something to give us a better idea of the character of the men at the head of the Government. Miss P. is always appealing to me in the History Class to enlighten them on subjects my ignorance of which I barely manage to conceal. When Miss P. asked who was the Prime Minister of England, not a voice, save my own was raised to reply, and on going out of class one girl asked me with a mystified air 'what a Prime Minister was?'

"School is almost over for this term, and I have almost concluded to stay in the Seminary except a day or two which I shall spend in Amherst. We will have a large Thanksgiving party on Thursday, as many of the teachers will not go away till after that. If I can persuade Fannie to stay we will have a very pleasant time.

"My lessons demand my attention now, and hoping soon to have time for a longer chat,

"I am your loving Daughter,

"ANNIE G. JOHNSON. "

---

" Nov. 24, 1868.

" DARLING ONES AT HOME,

"Vacation has come at last, or will be here to-morrow. These last days have been so very busy that I have hardly had a moment for writing. I believe I told you that I expect to stay in the Seminary, all, except a day or two, of vacation. There will be about twenty-five here, not including Miss S., Miss H. and Miss T., teachers who expect to remain ; so we will probably have a very pleasant time.

" The new series commenced to-day. My studies are Chemistry and Astronomy, and I have to attend two courses of lectures ; one in Natural Philosophy and the other in Chemistry, by Professors Snell and Porter, respectively. Chemistry will probably be very hard—we use Stockhardt's. H. D., of Marsowan, Turkey, and Ada F.,

K

of Tennessee, daughter of the Secretary of State, are my room-mates; we are all to be congregated in the South Wing, instead of being scattered in the four corners of this wilderness house.

"We have been preparing for Thanksgiving to-day, as that comes to-morrow. After working hard all the morning, I went on an excursion with Miss B. (my dear section teacher), and did not get back till supper time; consequently I am rather tired this evening.

"We are to have some kind of an entertainment to-morrow evening, at which I have to play of course.

"It is very pleasant to think of this two weeks' rest from study: You can hardly imagine how we delight in our release from rules. Hattie and I have just been proposing to find our way to the village prayer meeeting, if we can get permission to go out in the evening. The rules to which we have yet to submit are—Absence from, or tardiness at table; taking food from the basement; going out in the evening; riding without permission, and going out of town.

"Well, good-night darlings, write soon to your forlorn
                                                "ANNIE."

                                        "Dec. 10th, 1868.

" DEAR PAPA,

        " According to agreement I went over to Amherst on Monday, intending to return on Wednesday morning. The Agricultural Convention held its annual session in Amherst at the same time, so there were several distinguished persons present. Mr. R. came from New York, bringing Prof. G. from London, England, to stay at Mrs. W's. Prof. G. is a tall, handsome Englishman, and expects to obtain a seat in Parliament soon.

But, papa, I've heard *Prof. Agassiz*; the renowned *Agassiz*. As he was to lecture on Wednesday evening, my friends urged me to stay, but fearing I would be 'tardy in returning' on Thursday morning. I reluctantly but positively refused; however, Mr. H., the father of one of my school-mates, sent word that if I would stay he would bring me to the Sem. with his daughter in good time on Thursday morning. Of course I stayed then. The subject of the lecture was the formation of the soil, or the changes produced on the earth by the action of glaciers. It was *deep* and *dry*, but interesting because it came from Prof. Agassiz's lips. He is a rather short man, with a face of German roundness, and has a very broad German accent. He very seldom lectures, and it is not probable that I will ever have another chance to hear him, so that I do not at all regret staying, especially as we got back to the Sem. in good time this morning.

" My two room-mates are here, and I feel glad to be in school again. After my early sleigh-ride this morning I feel very tired and cannot answer now M's letter, which came this evening. I have heard no rumor of the death of the French Emperor, but the fact of his unpopularity makes it seem not improbable.

" Yours lovingly,

" ANNIE."

" Dec. 23rd, 1868.

" DARLING M.,

"Only two days before Christmas ! How *can* I keep from being homesick. My two room-mates have been sadly afflicted with this complaint for some days, and perhaps the necessity for one comforter in the room, was the reason of my escape. We will probably have a half holiday, but no more.

" My studies are very delightful. Chemistry is comparatively easy now, but we are to have lectures every day after Christmas, and then the trouble will be to find time for all our work. But oh ! Astronomy is delightful. It requires hard and patient study, with much thought, but how richly we are rewarded for it.

" It is hard to divest our minds of the incorrect ideas about the universe, which we have unconsciously cherished, but as on study and reflection the wonderful system is comprehended, it is impossible not to be impressed and awed by the evidences of some mighty Power ruling supreme in the ' celestial vault.'

" Then astronomers afford such bright examples of what steady perseverance and unwearied application can accomplish.

" The great Kepler searched incessantly eight long years for his ' First Law,' now comprised in two lines of our Astronomy. The third was revealed to him as the reward of seventeen years, patient toil.

" Well, dear, is this enough of Astronomy ? We must trace constellations together when I go home.

" Thank you for sending me Farmer's Mass; it came in time.   You ought to hear its grand harmonies ; I had no idea such a treasure was lying silent and neglected among our music.

" Well, darling sister, I must close this short letter.   I think of you all, *all the time.*

" Love to all the darling ones, and a merry, merry Christmas, from

" Your most loving<br>" ANNIE."

---

" DEC 29th, 1868.

" DARLING ONES AT HOME,

"Christmas has come and  gone, and at last I find a moment in which to give you  some idea of the day as spent in the Seminary.

" Mamma's and M's letters  came to me on Christmas eve, and oh! how  delighted I  was to get them.  The money was such a welcome gift; so many thanks for it.

" Christmas day was a *whole* holiday.  Observe, M., the stride in civilisation since you were here.  We all had a sleigh drive; then in the afternoon our class practised gymnastics for the benefit of the school and visitors; we did ourselves credit, I assure you.  From five o'clock till supper (at half-past seven) we remained in the gaily decorated Seminary  hall, amusing ourselves with  games and music.  Mr. Greene was there, and entered into our games as heartily as a school boy.  After supper we returned and remained till nine.  Deacon Kimball, whom you probably remember well, sent a quantity of little books, nicely bound in brown and written by himself, to be given to us. Beside this, I found in my boot a candy dog, horse and man, though from my slight acquaintance with natural history I failed at first to distinguish between them. F's share in the munificent gift may be seen from an item in her account book, reading—' One man of sweetness—one cent.'

" Of course the section teachers received presents as usual. We gave Miss B. the ' Life of Michael Angelo ' in two handsome volumes, with which she was sincerely delighted. We, the gymnastic classes, also gave Miss M. who is to be married very soon, a handsome silver fruit dish, breakfast castor, and a silver spoon.

" I'm waiting for a pen and ink description of your Christmas. Can it be a year since I spent that day in Ottawa ; as I look back on 1868 it seems shorter than any year I ever spent.

" There is to be an eclipse of the moon in January, and of the sun next August, that will be in my summer vacation.

" Will you have union meetings after New Year's ? M. dear, you must feel some affection for the Seminary after spending a year here, and as the day comes for special prayer for colleges, will you not remember us especially ?

" It is so pleasant to have two nice room-mates, more so than I thought it could be.

" Good night, darling ones

" Yours  lovingly,
" ANNIE G. J."

"February 25, 1869.

"DARLING SISTER A.,

"You cannot think how glad I was to get your letter just the day after M.'s. You are improving in your handwriting, and I noticed a good many more commas than you usually put in your letters; see if you cannot employ some semi-colons also, in your next letter. M. will tell you where they ought to be used.

"I wish you could be here these beautiful days. I never saw a winter scene so beautiful as met the gazers from our cupola yesterday morning. As the sun rose over Prospect Hill his splendor was flashed back by myriads of crystal objects. Every tree seemed laden with gems, and everywhere the pure white crust was studded with sparkling diamonds. It was such a scene as is seldom witnessed, and I shall not soon forget it. There was some nice skating yesterday also, and we improved it to the best of our ability.

"Your own Sister,
"ANNIE."

"March 16, 1869.

"DARLING SISTER A.,

"To-day I got a letter from a precious little girl, directed all by herself. You can guess, can you not, who prepared such a pleasure for me? You were a darling to write me another letter so soon, and I assure you I was delighted to notice the nice writing and the improved punctuation. Persevere, darling, and you will soon know all about how to write a letter.

"Yes, pet, it does seem too good to be true.  One week from to-morrow, on Thursday evening, I expect to start; and then how soon I will be driving up to our door, perhaps with you and M. beside me, and mamma's brown eyes in the doorway.  Oh! you darlings, just think of it.

---

"March, 1869.

"A., PRECIOUS,

"My heart was made glad on Saturday night, by the receipt of two letters from you and one from M.

"A dear little robin is building a nest in a tree outside of our window.  Don't you wish you could watch him as he works?

"Is papa going to raise some tomatoes this summer. I am longing for some to eat.  How much maple sugar is there in Canada?  Not that I desire an exact estimate of the quantity; I merely enquire whether it is more or less plentiful than usual.

"Maple sugar reminds me that we had supper this evening, and from that I am led to the reflection that we heard some funny stories told.  Our conversation happened to turn upon the subject of amusing and embarrassing accidents in church, and Miss B. related a little story about her grandfather, as an illustration.  It seems that he was a farmer, and became so wearied with the duties of the work, that he frequently fell asleep in church. On one occasion he was thus calmly reposing, when the minister, growing more vehement in his expressions, made use of some sudden exclamation. The venerable sleeper was deluded with the thought that he was in his farm wagon, and that this exclamation was a call from one of his men. Accordingly, in his anxiety to listen, he burst forth in stentorian tones, 'Whoa! Gee!! Whoa!!!' and thereafter was never caught napping.

"A's *great* grandfather was now called up for our amusement. He was a good, earnest Christian, but timid, and could never be induced to 'speak in meeting,' though convinced that this was his duty. Many were his mental conflicts, and severe his self-accusations; but one night in a certain meeting, after inwardly debating for some time, he resolved that he *would* try, no matter what it might cost him. It happened that a lady was speaking, but in so faint a tone that he did not hear her; accordingly, when the decision was made in his own mind, he rose to his feet and ejaculated with decision, '*Down* Satan! I will speak!!' to the great discomfiture of the lady who immediately obeyed the command, and sank into her seat.

"Many other stories were told, but these will serve as examples. Miss B. fears that we at her table are getting too sober, and tries once in a while to induce a hearty laugh, as an aid to digestion.

----

" Wednesday morning.

" At a time denoted by the cessation of the rising bell, I sit down to finish my letter.

" This is a lovely morning,. and we will probably have a *very* warm day.

" So you have quite decided that I shall stay home for the next year, have you ?  Well, child, I'll see.

" I have concluded not to study Theology this summer, but to have an easy time with only two familiar studies, and then we will all enjoy studying Natural Theology together at home.  It is very easy and delightful.

" Have you found many flowers yet ?  You will press every new kind you find, will you not ? especially if you find yellow violets, press a nice specimen.

" Well darling, I have written quite as long as I ought to.  You will write very soon, won't you ?  With loads of love, I am,

" Your own Sister,

" Annie."

---

" April 19th, 1869.

" A., My Pet,

" I was delighted to find your letter and M's waiting for me as I came in this evening.  I wish I had time to send you a long letter, but the evenings are so short that I can do very little.

" We too, darling, have lovely, charming weather ; for the past few days it has been so warm that we felt like putting on muslins.  ' Snow,' indeed ! Why the grass is green, and in many places the flowers are in bloom. There is a darling little patch of pink blossoms down in the court.

" In obedience to the imperative call of ' duty,' I pro-

ceed to report on my state of health.  With all truthfulness, I can say that it has very much improved; my cold
is disappearing rapidly, and I am thoroughly delighted
with summer prospects.

" We have just commenced the study of Hebrews.  It
is very interesting indeed.  For this morning our lesson
consisted in finding proofs of its ' Pauline origin,' as Miss
S. terms it.  The sunlight in our room worked wonders
for F.  She is quite well now, and has commenced attending her recitations."

———

" Six O'clock, Wednesday Morning.

" Last night Messrs. Stocking and Ford delivered a lecture, or rather gave us an entertainment in the Seminary
hall.  Mr. S. is a Senior and Mr. F. a Freshman in Wil-
liams' College.  They are sons of missionaries, and preparing for the same work themselves.  They have not
been in this country very long, and are thoroughly acquainted with the lands of whose customs they tell us.

" Mr. S., from Persia, addressed us first.  His manner
was very good, showing no signs of the verdancy we expected to see in so young a lecturer.  His lecture consisted of a narration of incidents in a journey to his home, all
intended to give us an idea of the people and customs of
the country.  He described the Nestorians who are among
the lower classes of the people, and gave the call to
prayer in that language.  His description of the wedding
ceremony was quite amusing; an important part of it

consisting in the greeting of the loving bridegroom, who goes up on the housetop, when the bridal party comes in sight, armed with six large apples, which he hurls one by one at the head of his veiled bride. If he succeeds in hitting her several times, it is a good omen, if he fails altogether he has reason to expect domestic trials.

" Mr. Stocking's speech was quite short, and when he closed, he introduced to us Mr. Ford, only two years from Palestine. Mr. Ford, more boyish looking than his companion, had an entirely different way of speaking. He spoke rapidly, and yet so clearly as to keep one's attention fixed. His endeavor was to show us life in the village in Palestine where his home was.

" The houses are all built up on the sloping hillside in such a way that the roof of one forms a large platform before the front door of the one above it. They consist of one room, one wall of which is simply the rocky hill against which it is built. The roof is of mud, straw, thorny brush and clay. After the clay is hardened by the sunlight, it cracks, and then leaves convenient places for the entrance of the rain ; also, as the roofs are used as promenades by men and quadrupeds, the material of which the roof is formed sifts down continually, forming a pleasant admixture with the food and rendering constant diligence in the use of the comb necessary.

" The children are a great annoyance to the Americans as they follow them in the streets, hooting and jabbering after them. An Englishman was much incensed by this treatment, and took a novel way of ridding himself of such annoyance. As the children cried after him, he manifested great delight, exclaiming, 'I like that ; do it again, won't you ? *Do* go on, I enjoy it so much ! Won't you say that every time I come out ? I would'nt have you stop for anything, I'll tell you what I will do, if you'll promise to continue it, I'll give each of you two cents every time you do it ! ' The avaricious beings were 'of course delighted, and shouted at him with renewed energy ; and so it continued for a few days, when the Englishman called them to him and said he could'nt afford to pay them any longer, in fact ' he would *not* pay them.' The urchins demurred very much at this ; declared that it was quite too much trouble to screech at him for nothing, and they *would not* do it unless he paid them. He remained steadfast and they troubled him no more.

"Mr. Ford told us a great many very amusing stories in a very amusing way, but I have not now time to recount them. He gave us all much valuable information ; explained many prophetical allusions, and the customs with which it was necessary to be acquainted in order to understand all the parables.

"As he concluded his speech, Mr. Stocking appeared on the platform, arrayed in the common dress of the Persians. His black, conical-shaped cap rose a foot and more over his head. His coat seemed to be made of some green material like cotton ; it was long, and fastened at the waist with a voluminous sash. The sleeves, at first sight, appeared to be in a very ragged condition, but we found that they were made so purposely, in accordance with

'the latest fashion.' The trousers were large bags
drawn closely round the ankles. He kept the dress on
during the remainder of the evening, and looked like
some poverty-stricken piece of misery. Mr. Ford went
out, and shortly we heard a great stamping which pre-
luded the appearance of an Arab on stilts. Here was our
youthful lecturer transformed into a fierce looking Arab
with a most becoming black moustache clinging to his
upper lip. This dress was much more elegant than the
other, and the wearer explained it in a very amusing
manner. Taking up a white cap worn inside of a
black one, he said, 'This is worn for the sake of cleanli-
ness; is frequently washed; in fact some have been known
to wash it *once a year*. With the help of his colleague,
he enveloped himself in a sheet to show us how the
women always look on the street. Then he sang for us a
lugubrious song with which the girls beguile the time
when they are guiding the plough. But oh! could you
have heard the melodious strains which he drew from a
flute such as the shepherd boys use, you might, as an ac-
companiment to E's melancholy resignation of the fiddle,
hang your harp upon the willows. Both young men had
very pleasing voices and sang two pieces together, one in
Syriac and the other in Arabic. They were truly beautiful.

"A small table, half a foot high, was set out in the
middle of the platform, and at this they soon sat down.
The table was furnished with a little tin teapot containing cold water; two or three thin, flat cakes of bread, and

a bowl of rice. The repast seemed not to be very tempting, as it was very sparingly patronized. The youths went through the oriental salutations, consisting of various bowings and scrapings, and finished by a kiss on each cheek."

------

" Wednesday Evening.

" You see, darling, that this is still unfinished, though I fear your patience is quite exhausted now. We were delighted with the evening's entertainment, and so glad that we could do anything to assist such worthy young men.

" Your very loving Sister,

" ANNIE."

------

Nearly nineteen years have passed away since she who wrote the foregoing letters, was called to relinquish the studies in which she took such delight, to pursue a higher course in the "Father's House, above."

Her life, from her earliest childhood, was characterized by unselfishness, and helpfulness to others. These characteristics were strengthened by her life at Mt. Holyoke seminary, where "not for ourselves" is the noble life-motto held up before its pupils.

It was constantly a source of thankfulness to Annie's mother, ever solicitous for the highest welfare of her children, that her eldest daughter had learned what it was to "redeem the time;" that, at an age, when so many young ladies are engaging with such zest, and with such injury to themselves, in a life of gaiety and fashion, her loved one's bright youth was devoted to the cultivation of her talents for future usefulness; that she had learned, though so young, that life and youth and health, and powers of mind, were all so many sacred trusts to be improved for God.

Her life gave promise of being one of great usfulness, as, added to her industry, studiousness and religious principle, was an unfailing fund of good spirits and energy. Her health was almost always good, and she did not suffer from the nervousness and depression which is so common with young persons of an apparently less vigorous constitution. But all unaware to herself, as well as to her friends, she overtaxed her strength during the last year at school. Her parents, fearing lest she might have done this, persuaded her to consent to a year's rest from such constant study, and she came home for her summer vacation in 1869 with the prospect, delightful to herself and family, of having a long, happy year with her loved ones, after which (for she never failed to keep this in view) she would return to the Seminary for the fourth and last year, to graduate.

But a better vocation was in store for our darling; a longer rest than any of us anticipated; a brighter home was to be hers, while for us, the light of life was to become suddenly strangely darkened; earthly things were to crumble as we grasped them, and heaven become the spot where our best affections were centred.

Six or seven short weeks of happy life with the family, united save for the absence of one son, elapsed, and then she was seized with a sudden, resistless fever. Fragments of Latin, or troublesome mathematical problems repeated by her in her delirium, shewed the condition of the overwrought brain, and after an illness of less than one week she passed away.

Over that sorrow let us draw a veil. Even after the lapse of so many years, the mind does not dare to dwell upon the awfulness of that blow as seen from its earthly side. He, who "healeth the broken in heart" was wonderfully present to comfort, and the dear mother, whose physical strength was completely prostrated by the shock, was yet the comfort and stay of the whole family. She was enabled almost to pierce the veil which intervened between the two worlds, and to rejoice in the new and fuller and perfect life upon which her loved one had entered. Through all, the bereaved parents were enabled to look up and to recognize the voice which said to them :—

"BE STILL, AND KNOW THAT 1 AM GOD."

The following letters written by her mother not long after this bereavement, contain details as to Annie's life during the few weeks after her return from school, and of the circumstances attending her death :—

"OTTAWA, Oct. 9th, 1869.

"MY DEAR MISS W.,

"You will doubtless, ere this, have heard of the death of our dear Annie, nevertheless I feel it right to

L

communicate with you on the subject, and have been only waiting to gain sufficient strength to write yon.

"My darling had hardly passed the period of her vacation, when she was suddenly snatched away from our sight. I, her mother, had not even the privilege of watching her in her last hours. On a visit at Toronto, I did not get word of her danger till it was too late.

"She was taken (as it was thought) *slightly* ill on Sunday, the 5th September, and fell asleep in Jesus on the Saturday following. No one apprehended any danger until Thursday, when she became delirious. There is no doubt that her constant application to her studies, in addition to many other engagements into which she voluntarily entered, laid the foundation of the disease which took her from us.

"Dear child—to us she was everything we could wish; the most affectionate and dutiful of daughters, the most unselfish and loving sister, and a warm friend to her companions at school. Dare I for a moment consider this event as human nature would picture it to me, I should be overwhelmed with grief. But I have been shown that hers is a glorious destiny, that she has been called to a state where she can prosecute her studies without any hindrance such as she met with here; where she can engage in acts of benevolence, and be a ministering spirit to those she loves; where her soul expands with raptures, at the prospect which stretches out before her of illimitable progress and ever new delights. Oh I have been so comforted, and so filled with delight and thankfulness to God that I had such a treasure to present to Him.

'It was on account of the religious character of the school that we were induced to send our daughter thither, and we never felt any regret that we had chosen that place; on the contrary, I feel more and more grateful to God for the advantages which that school afforded, and for the variety of interests which are included in its routine.

----

" OTTAWA, Oct. 24th, 1869.

" MY DEAR SISTER,

" I received your kind sympathising letter, and will now attempt to give you a more detailed account of our darling's sickness and death.

" Precious one ! She was so delighted with the prospect of remaining home a year, and we were all rejoicing in the same prospect. She came home on the 18th of July, apparently in her usual good health, though I could not but perceive she was a little thinner, a very little thinner, and there was a worn look about her eyes. But she told us how very much hurried she had been in her last term at school, and she, as well as we, thought that a rest of a few weeks was all she required. She complained of nothing, and was as ready as ever to enter into every scheme that was set on foot, either to promote the interests of the family or the community.

" My reasons for resolving to have her home this year were, first, that she might have more leisure to engage in work for those objects in which we are interested, in company with us—and secondly, that there might be no

danger to her health for want of rest from study.    I had
sent her word sometime previous to her return, to  bring
all her things home, as I was resolved she must not  go
back this year.    She readily assented, and had the ap-
proval of her teachers, who had advised several of  the
senior middlers to remain out a year ; though Annie was
thought quite strong enough to go straight through  the
course.

" She came home in the best of spirits, and filled  with
thankfulness, which she often expressed, that she had
'such a lovely home.'   Dear one !   It was lovely while she
was with us, and it was so before because of the  love
which we all felt for her, and each other.    How she felt
for those girls in the school who would as soon spend their
vacations away from home, as with their own  parents—
she could not understand it.    Often had some of  her
schoolmates said to her, ' I envy you your happy home.'

" About a fortnight after she arrived home, I went with
her, T. and M., to spend a few days at Chelsea, to  enjoy
the mountain air, and to ramble among the rocks and beside the lakes.    That was a pleasure which I shall never
forget, as it was the last trip or  excursion  we can  ever
have with her on earth.    I never shall forget her quiet
happiness when she would find beautiful ferns and  rare
plants, for the collecting of which she had, before  we
went, procured a tin botanical box.

" Shortly after our return home, most of us took severe
colds ; dear Annie's cough was very bad, but she  kept
herself busy, always employed about others, regardless of

herself.  Often I begged her to lay aside what she was
doing, and she would promise to do so, as soon as she had
finished, etc., etc.  Her cold gradually appeared to leave
her, and about seven weeks after our loved one came
home, M. and I went to Toronto.  I had no fear on the
ground of sickness at home, having left directions that
we should hear every day, and be telegraphed for, if all
were not well.  I arrived at my friend's in Toronto on
Saturday morning—the *following Saturday I reached
home again, eight hours after my precious one had fallen
asleep in Jesus.*

"What do you think I felt ?  What did M. feel ?  We
were all bound up in that dear one, and there she lay !

"My dear sister, it seems to me one of the greatest
wonders in the world, that event—nothing will ever seem
so strange to me.  What would an earthquake be, or an
armed force ?  I do not know, but all things are changed
with us, so that what was once a source of apprehension,
is nothing now.

"You will ask, how did it happen that you did not
know of her illness in time to get home ?  I will tell you.
M. and I had left home on Friday.  On the following
Sunday Annie was poorly and did not go out all day, but
lay on the sofa.  In the evening her father called in a
physician, though he did not think her seriously ill.  The
doctor was in attendance every day, during her brief illness.  On Monday my husband wrote me a letter, which
I did not receive till Wednesday, in which he said not a
word about her illness, and told me I had better prolong

my visit.    How was this ?    Dearest one, she and all, the
doctor included, thought she would be well in a few days,
and feared that it would interfere with our comfort, and
curtail our visit, if we should hear of her *slight indispo-
sition.*

" It was not until Wednesday night that they became
alarmed about her, and then it was too late to send a telegram.

" She began to be delirious, as fever developed.   As
early as possible in the morning a despatch was sent to
me, but it did not reach the house in which I was staying till about ten minutes after I had started on the train
for Suspension Bridge.   (How it appeared as if the Lord
*determined* to keep me away from that scene.)   It was
not until our arrival at the Bridge that we received the
telegram.   It was then five o'clock in the afternoon, and
we learned, to our dismay, that there was no train back
till the morning.   So we had to endure the suspense of
remaining there all night, going back to Toronto the next
day, and then home on Saturday.

" The telegram contained the words : ' Return immediately, wanted at home, Annie sick.'

" It was wonderful how I was enabled to give up that
precious treasure on that very night, yet I hoped I should
not be put to the test.   I wondered at myself that I
could with all my heart give her up to the will of her
loving Saviour.

" We were from Thursday night until Saturday afternoon in ignorance about her state.   I was ill myself with

a kind of fever that lasted for a fortnight after I came home. When we arrived at the station in Ottawa, instead of T. or his father meeting us, an acquaintance called a cab for us, and handed us in.

"I did not dare to ask a question, but a friend who had joined us on our journey from Prescott, and who was behind us, asked the friend who had taken us in charge, ' Do you know how Miss Johnson is ? '

" She was very ill, last night," was the reply.

" I felt inwardly impatient at the evasive answer, and yet hoped that he would say no more. Presently a lady friend appeared, and began talking to me, asked how I was, etc.

" I said I was not at all well, had heard bad news from home. 'Did you not hear' said I 'that my daughter is very ill ? '

"' O yes,' said she.

"' How is she now ? ' I ventured at last to ask.

"' She was very ill last night.'

"' But oh ! tell me—how is she now ? '

"' *She is well now.*'

" Poor M., she did not hear this, but she knew from my appearance all about it.

" We had a silent, strange drive home ; found Papa, T. and A. just as might have been expected ; worn out with watching, desolate and amazed.

" The most wonderful part remains to be told, and that is the miraculous way in which I was sustained, and the strong conviction that came to my mind that every circumstance was ordered by Infinite Wisdom, so that I could not regret anything. For some days I was in a state of joy, more complete than I had ever known. If my dear one had been restored to me just as she was when I left her standing at the front door the morning I left home—when I looked upon her for the last time—I could not have felt more joyful. I had such a view of the wisdom and love of God in taking her to Himself; such a firm persuasion that she was taken away in order to prosecute the work she so ardently wished to accomplish; such a vivid view of the *fact* that she was in every way capable of doing for us what her loving, affectionate disposition inclined her to desire, as I never can describe. I would not have called her back to earth for the world.

"I witnessed all the preparations for her funeral, saw the people coming to the house, heard (but not distinctly, for I kept my room) the prayers, saw from my window the coffin placed in the hearse, the long line of coaches that followed those precious remains, and never grieved any more than I should have done had I seen her going to church, accompanied by cheerful friends, expecting her back in an hour.

"I cannot explain this, but have realized what I feel to be the greatest miracle, and it has given me a greater idea of the power of God than I ever had before.

"It is now five weeks and two days since our loved one went to Heaven. We had spoken several times about moving from the house we then occupied during the few weeks of her sojourn with us, and she was well pleased

with the idea of the change. We did not, however, decide
fully about moving until after she fell asleep—I cannot
say *died*. It is just a week to-day since we left the place
where we resided ever since coming to Ottawa. There
was one thing I thought I should regret, and that was
not being able to go into the room where the dear one
had breathed her life away, but that is made up to me
by the fact which I was astonished to learn, that we can
see her grave from our windows. You may think this a
strange source of comfort, but I am so thankful that I
can look out every morning from my bedroom window
and see the grave * of my bright, sweet, loving Annie,
the most affectionate and dutiful of daughters.

"Do not think that life has lost its sweetness to us.
Oh no! We want to live to do the work assigned to us,
so as to meet again with joy our darling, who is now, I
believe, permitted to be near us in this life of probation.

"I could write much more and tell you how thankful I
am for the way in which part of every day was spent by
us after our darling came home, and how her religious
character had developed, how lovely her whole deportment was, how unselfish, how assiduous in her attention
to us all. Thank our blessed Lord, she is forever happy
and blest.

"Your loving Sister,

"A. B. JOHNSON."

---

* The body was afterwards removed to Beechwood Cemetery.

"He leadeth me beside the still waters."

Twenty summers passed and ended,
  Like a fleeting April ray—
Part with us and part in Heaven,
  Resting till the Judgment Day.

Here, the tall trees casting shadows ;
  Here, the sunset gilded wave ;
Here, her form we loved so dearly ;
  Here her quiet Christian grave.

There, the placid streams of comfort,
  Watering many a verdant lea ;
There, the spirit that has left us,
  Waiting till the end shall be.

Here, the great unrest of ages ;
  Here, the trouble, toil, and strife ;
There, the peaceful, quiet waters
  Of the crystal stream of life.

Here, the sighing of the branches ;
  Here, the wave-beat on the shore ;
There, the ceaseless strain of angels
  Chanting praises evermore.

Here, the rocks, and shoals, and quicksands ;
  Here, the white cross on the sod ;
There, the heaven where she would be,
  In the bosom of her God.

                    —B. COURTENAY GIDLEY.

## VI.

IT is fitting that the foregoing letters should be followed by some account of the eldest son, who surveved his sister scarcely four years.

At the time of his death a short obetuary was written by the late Canon Johnston, and this is here re-produced, with the introduction, in which the parents of the young clergyman presented the memorial to his parishioners.

---

## INTRODUCTION.

THE following memorial, kindly furnished by the most intimate friend and father in the ministry of their dear son—in connection with the singularly appropriate sermon, the manuscript of which he had evidently been studying as he travelled in the discharge of his duty to his Divine Master, when so suddenly called to "exchange mortality for life," and which was found beside his body, slightly stained with his blood—is presented to his parishoners and friends by his bereaved parents, with the prayer and in the earnest hope, that the lessons taught so clearly, and Providentially inculcated by the painful circumstances, may be the means, under the Divine blessing, of leading many to thoughtfulness and prayer.

OTTAWA CITY,
    *27th August,* 1873.

# OBITUARY.

"What I say unto you I say unto all—WATCH."

THESE words of our blessed Lord are presented with peculiar force to our minds in connection with the solemn warning we all have received in the sudden and most unexpected death of our dear departed brother, the REV THOMAS JOHNSON, Minister of the Church of England in Bristol, on the Ottawa. He had exchanged services for the day (the 17th of August) with a neighboring clergyman, and in the fulfilment of his duty he had to perform Divine Service in two townships, Leslie and Thorne. While proceeding from the former to the latter place to hold his second service, his horse ran away, throwing him out of the little spring cart in which he was driving, and, falling with fearful violence upon a projecting stone in the road, his skull was fractured, and his death was instantaneous. At the moment of his death, he was reading the last page of the sermon which he was on the eve of preaching to the congregation in Thorne. It was on the subject of death, and the importance of being prepared for that solemn event; and from the concluding words of his manuscript it is evident that he purposed closing the discourse with a solemn exhortation to his hearers to seek and secure Divine Grace, to fit them for death and judgment.

The deceased, whose career of usefulness has thus so early and suddenly closed on earth, was a man of far more than ordinary intellectual power.

Gentle and retiring in his manners, humble and diffident as to his own capabilities, those only who knew him well, or who happened to be with him when circumstances required him to throw off his usual diffidence, became aware of the varied information, the logical power, the quickness of conception, with which he would illustrate the subject in hand, and this in language always chaste and forcible.

From the time of his ordination to the sacred office of the ministry, and more especially for the last few months of his earthly career, Mr. JOHNSON was deeply, and even painfully, impressed with a sense of the awful responsibility of his sacred office. The portion of the mission field in which he laboured required at his hands many sacrifices, and much hard work, and when the writer of these few memorial lines reminded him that the Bishop spoke of appointing him to a more inviting field, and when he was urged to address the Bishop on the subject, the answer he gave was to the effect that he did not wish to write or mention the subject at all to his Bishop, that he felt the responsibility of his work so keenly that he shrunk from doing or saying anything to influence the mind of the Bishop in favor of his removal. That he wished to go wherever he was sent, and labour wherever he was appointed, and that he could thus more clearly recognize the directing hand of God's Providence in his work. That if his work was harder, and his discouragements greater than they were, he was quite prepared to labour on so long as he was appointed to that sphere of labour. He said, moreover, that the welfare of the souls of those among whom his work was being done, was daily becoming more and more his desire.

The last time he visited the writer of these few lines of affectionate remembrance, the subject of conversation turned upon death and the nature and condition of the spirit of man when separated from its earthly tabernacle; its probable surpise in realizing the perfection of its own identity; its complete possession of its faculties of memory, will, judgment, affections, powers of perception, and holding intercourse with other intelligent beings around it; its remembrances of friends on earth, as well as its recognition of those in paradise.

Little did the writer think that in a few days the dear friend with whom he was then conversing on those delightful topics would know so well from actual experience how far our conclusions were in accordance with the facts.

Now he is gone—the young, the wise, and the useful minister of Christ. May his unexpected departure speak to us the importance of "working while it is day," remembering that "the night cometh when no man can work."

His funeral was a solemn sight. Six clergymen in white surplices were the pall bearers, and six more also in their white robes preceded the coffin from his father's residence on Daly street to St. Alban's Church. There the solemn and beautiful burial service of the Church was offered. Twelve clergymen in their altar robes occupied their places in the Chancel, and united with the choir and congregation in the appropriate chants and hymns. Among the latter was the favorite hymn of the deceased:

> " Oh Paradise, O Paradise
> Who doth not crave for rest ?
> Who would not seek the happy land
> Where they that loved are blest ?
> Where loyal hearts and true
> Stand ever in the light,
> All rapture through and through,
> In God's most holy sight.
>
> O Paradise, O Paradise,
> 'Tis weary waiting here ;
> I long to be where Jesus is,
> To feel, to see him near ;
> Where loyal hearts and true
> Stand ever in the light,
> All rapture through and through,
> In God's most holy sight.
>
> O Paradise, O Paradise,
> I greatly long to see
> The special place my dearest Lord
> In love prepares for me ;

Where loyal hearts and true
Stand ever in the light,
All rapture through and through.
In God s most holy sight.

Lord Jesus, King of Paradise ;
O keep me in thy love,
And guide me to that happy land
Of perfect rest above ;
Where loyal hearts and true
Stand over in the light,
All rapture through and through,
In God's most holy sight."

To his sorrowing family, and indeed to all his friends, it is a source of great comfort to know that he met his death in the discharge of his sacred duty to his Divine Lord and Master.

Happy is it that his dear parents, whom he loved so much, and whose hearts clung to him with such intense affection, and looked forward to his future usefulness with such fond hope, know so well to whom they can go for comfort. Thank God they are enabled in this dark hour of trial, to say in the spirit of true resignation and Christian faith, " The Lord gave and the Lord hath taken away. Blessed be the name of the Lord."

O may we all be found at our post of duty, working, watching, looking for the Lord when the summons comes to us. May it be our happy lot to join our dear departed friend at last in the kingdom of our Lord, where death can never come, and sorrow and sighing flee away forever.

Where in the enjoyment of the Divine presence, in the associations of the blessed inhabitants of heaven, and in the eternal advancement in knowledge and happiness, we shall learn to prize more, and be more and more grateful for the infinite love of God, who in His mercy rescued us from the ruins of sin, and bestowed upon us this eternal felicity through the atonement of His own dear Son.

JOHN JOHNSTON,
*Minister St. James' Church, Hull.*

# SERMON.

---

*I am glad for your sakes that I was not there, to the intent ye may believe.*—JOHN xi, 15.

To most men death is a theme of sadness, if not of terror. We shrink from it, and yet how constantly and vividly is it kept in our view. Every day we are reminded that we are mortal. " All flesh is grass, and all the goodness of it as the flower of grass. The grass withereth, the flower fadeth." even so must everything earthly. All that is brightest and fairest must wither and fade and die. We walk through the valley of the shadow of death; that dark figure stands at the head of the way before us, and we walk ever in the gloomy shadow which it casts. It is natural that the thought of death should be one of gloom and even fear. We know that its coming is certain, but the day or the hour of its coming no man can tell. It sets at nought all human calculations estimates and probabilities. It is indiscriminate in its ravages; it takes the young as well as the old, the good as well as the bad; it spares not for human terror and sorrow, but tears away the stay of the feeble, the hope of nations, the good, the brave, the promising. And then it is a mystery; the grave is clothed with darkness; it is a change so sudden, so great, so incomprehensible.

No wonder that those who live by sight and not faith, should shrink from the contemplation of such a theme.

The narative from which our text is taken, presents the subject of death before us, but not as associated with gloom. Its brighter aspects are shown ; we are pointed to the lights 'in the picture as well as the shades; death is shorn of its terrors, and light gleams through the darkness of the tomb. It is a most affecting story, one that comes home to our own hearts. It is the oft-told story of human love and grief, of loss and desolation, and of Divine tenderness and care. It is full of instruction. Let us attempt to gather some of its lessons for our comfort and help, and the increase of our faith.

The first words of our Saviour in the text are remarkable. " I am glad." At this time Mary and Martha, dear friends of Jesus, were crushed with grief, and yet concerning the cause of their sorrow He said, " I am glad." This utterance must have sounded very strange to the disciples, for as yet they only knew Christ after the flesh, at least they had but a dim comprehension of the spiritual truths upon which His action was based. His character was still something of a riddle to their minds. Hence his expression was to them a mystery. We are learners in the school of life—we know the systen of truth revealed in God's word—we believe in Christ—we feel ourselves to be under the rule and care of God—we recognize the Lord Jesus Christ as our Saviour and Lord, but there is much in the Providence of God that is dark to us ; sin has weakened our spiritual eyesight, and our perceptions are clouded and dim.

The Christian, as he advances in his religious life, feels more and more his own inherent feebleness and ignorance, the imperfection and meagreness of his views, and feels more and more the absolute need of Divine enlightenment and counsel. The disciples could not understand the motives of Christ in allowing, when He might have prevented, the death of His friend, with all its consequences of sorrow to those who were left behind. This case is not a singular one. There are few in whose experience it has not been repeated. "God's ways are not as our ways." Many of His dealings with us are beyond human understanding. There are times when to the unaided human mind, it must seem as if God had withdrawn Himself from His creatures, and left them to suffer unheeded and uncared for—that He was deaf to the cry of human agony. Why does God thus hide Himself, as it were, and allow His creatures to suffer? If, with the disciples, we have thus questioned within our hearts, we shall find in the text the solution of the problem. In it are unfolded the purposes of God, and the principles of His government of men.

And 1st. Our Lord was glad for the sake of His disciples.

To have saved the life of Lazarus would have been more consistent with the views and wishes of His disciples. It would have been *apparently* more consistent with His regard for His friends. It would have saved them present pain. But His desire for His followers extended beyond their present happiness. His views and His actions had

reference to their highest welfare. He had regard to
their spiritual improvement—to their eternal well being.
There was a lesson in this calamity which they must
learn, even at the expense of pain to those who were so
dearly beloved. The whole life of our blessed Saviour
was a carrying out of this principle. All that He did
and suffered was for the sake of His Church. Did He
leave the Throne of Majesty in heaven—did He empty
Himself of glory, and take upon Himself the deepest
humiliation and abasement ?   " For our sakes He became
poor." Did He here endure sorrows and pain, more deep,
more intense than the human mind can conceive ?   " He
bore our griefs and carried our sorrows." Did He take
upon Himself the burden of a world's sin, and sanctify
Himself for the work of a Mediator ?   For our sakes He
did it, and that *we* might be sanctified by the truth.   A
voice from heaven comforted Him, and He said, "' This
voice came not because of me, but for your sakes.   After
having suffered He left the world, because " it was ex-
pedient for us that the Comforter might come to us."
And He now sitteth at the right hand of the Majesty on
high, that *we* may have " an Advocate with the Father.''
Upon the same law proceed His dealings with us, His
children.   It is the law of love, which regards not so
much the present happiness as the future blessedness of
its object.   Whatever befalls us then, whatever sorrows
reach us, however dark may seem the ways of God with
us, we know that it is for our sake, for our own good, that
it is from Him who loves us with an infinite love, who

for our sake spared not Himself, but freely gave Himself for us all.

Again. Our Lord was glad that He was not there—that is, to heal the sick. To have brought deliverance to that sorrowing family would have been a blessing—to withhold it was a greater blessing. By His presence, what comfort and joy would He have given to those hearts, now well nigh breaking with their agony of suspense and dread. They had sent to him, "Lord he whom thou lovest is sick." He knew how they longed for Him; His heart was with them. He saw the trouble that was falling upon them. He saw the dread shadow of death as it grew deeper and blacker, as it settled down upon them, throwing its gloom upon all their pleasant things, until it shut out all light and joy from their home, and yet He stayed away. Did they wonder at His absence, at His seeming indifference? Did they think that He had forsaken them? They were to learn that in this was a higher exercise of His love towards them than if He had responded to their prayer. In this, infinite love and wisdom were united to secure for them a blessing beyond what they could conceive. Doubtless many of us have known the bitterness of bereavement.

Unexpectedly in the midst of the business and enjoyment of life, sorrow has come upon us. As in southern lands, a cloudless sky is suddenly overcast, and the tempest comes down in might and terror; in our serenest hour the clouds have gathered, and the sudden storm has broken, crushing us with its overwhelming power and leaving us shattered and desolate. We shrank and cried out for succor as we saw the blow coming upon us; we refused to believe that relief would not come, and when the worst came we thought our grief greater than we could bear. Perhaps we murmured, feeling that God had dealt too heavily with us. Or we have seen the strange mysterious dealings of God with our neighbors. But far be it from us to judge the dispensations of God. We must wait. When the great plan of the Almighty is worked out—when His mighty purposes are accomplished, we shall see the end towards which these things are working. "God is unsearchable; His ways past finding out," but of one thing we may be sure, that all His plans are laid in wisdom and carried out in love—that if He cause sorrow, it is that we may partake more abundantly of His mercy. His wisdom is infinite, He cannot err; His love is infinite, He cannot be unkind.

"I am glad for your sake that I was not there, to the intent ye may believe."

Here the Lord explains the purpose for which He had allowed this affliction to befall His friends at Bethany. It was for the increase of the disciples' faith. This was the benefit that was to flow out of and counterbalance all that sorrow. Now the disciples had already believed, but their faith was weak. Christ designed its increase. They were but beginners in the knowledge of God—they were slow to learn—they needed "line upon line, precept upon precept." Christ was leading them along, step by step, to a higher knowledge, to clearer views of truth, to higher

conceptions of Himself, to deeper acquaintance with the
things of God, to higher and purer experience. He was
training them for the mighty work which they had to do,
and to this end it was necessary that their faith should
be confirmed and strengthened; for upon their faith depended their spiritual life, their power, their usefulness.
And this is God's purpose in His dealing with us—" to the
intent ye may believe." Faith is the foundation, the
beginning and the end of Christian life. By faith we are
justified—by faith we are sanctified—by faith we are
furnished unto good works. Faith then is the supreme
good. To believe is to achieve the chief end of existence.
To increase in faith is to advance towards the accomplish-
ment of the greater purpose of our life. Upon this depend eternal issues. In this pursuit are bound up all our
hopes and happiness; therefore the increase of our faith
is the most precious thing in the esteem of our Lord. In
His dealings with us it is His aim to keep this in our
remembrance. We are slow to learn—we are prone to
forget the aim of our creation—apt to lose sight of our
true pursuits, and to identify ourselves with earth until
we become earthly altogether. We live by *sight*, and not
by *faith*; therefore it is in compassion that God lays His
hand upon us; His chastisements are marks of love; the
sorrows He sends us are blessings; His judgments are
mercies; He deals with us as with sons. We cling to
earth until we are in danger of forgetting heaven,
and it is necessary to our eternal safety that
we should learn how vain and unsatisfying

are earthly things. If we will not learn it otherwise, we must learn it through disappointment, loss,
sorrow. Many a man has been first awakened to the uncertainty of earthly things by the overthrow of some
cherished hope 'or ambition; many a man has got his
first glimpse of heaven through the grave of some loved
one. And if we have strayed or are in danger of stray-
ing from the path of holiness, is anything too hard, if
only we may be brought back again? No, let us weep,
for we cannot help it when losses come upon us; but if
they awaken us to our need of God, if they bring us to a
truer and more abiding consciousness of eternity, if they
bring us into nearer communion with Christ, then we
have cause to rejoice even in our pain, and our rejoicing
will be eternal. Christ taught His disciples through the
sorrow of Mary and Martha. He speaks to us in the afflic-
tions of others. They are admonitions to us—they call us
to a recognition of our own frailty and His omnipotence.
We know not what a day or an hour may bring forth—
we know not what sorrow lies before us; let us heed the
voice of God—remember this is not our rest, and seek by
greater earnestness in our religious life to do and to bear
whatever may be God's will towards us.

Life is the time of probation and discipline; here we
are at school—our true life is hereafter. God would
draw our thoughts towards that higher and better life.
He would have us live in consciousness of eternal realities.
Anything that renders us more susceptible of the influences of the Holy Spirit—anything that impels us to-

wards Christ, that stirs up a truer and more practical recognition of our obligations and destiny, is a blessing. Any pain, any sorrow is worth enduring that shall arouse us from indifference or worldliness, that shall bring us into a state of humble and devout trust in God our Father.

Finally, we learn from the text that God does not willingly afflict, and that when trouble has accomplished its purpose relief comes. Jesus said, " Nevertheless let us go unto him." Jesus had seen all the conflict and sorrow in that home. His heart had been there, and now as soon as He could, consistently with the fulfilment of His high purpose, He went to them to bring comfort and relief. So it is still; our Saviour knows just how far it is necessary for us to be tried, and beyond that He will not try us. He is watching in tender love and compassion when His children suffer, and He is at hand to bind up their wounds, to still the storm of grief, and to pour consolation into the stricken hearts. He may not take away the cause of sorrow as in the case before us, but the succor He brings is none the less perfect. It only needs that we call upon Him. "Come unto me and I will give you rest," is the only source of relief. We may offer our sympathy to those who mourn—we may weep with those who weep, but how powerless are we to lessen the load of grief. How helpless we are in the presence of sorrow ; we can do nothing, but Christ can do all. There is no sorrow that He cannot heal ; His help is practical and efficient ; "cast thy burden upon the Lord and He will sustain thee." He will speak words of comfort ; He will impart strength ; He will point the crushed and despairing soul to the better land where the loved and lost are waiting until those who are left behind for a season shall meet them again ; the home of the soul where there is no more death ; "where the inhabitants never say they are sick ; where God shall wipe away all tears from off all faces." Christ can work for us a far more blessed deliverance than the removal of the present trouble. "This light affliction which is but for a moment, worketh for us a far more exceeding and eternal weight of glory." The troubles of life are light compared with the blessedness that God has prepared for them that love Him. If the wounded heart turns to Christ as its stay and refuge, and clings to Him with intenser love and firmer faith, then will it prove the blessedness of adversity. It shall dwell on high ; it shall abide under the shadow of the Almighty. God calls us to a higher life, a truer existence, a closer communication with Himself. "Eye hath not seen nor ear heard what God hath prepared for them that love Him," He would lift our souls to a higher plane, where they shall breathe a purer atmosphere, where in the sunlight of His countenance they shall become strong and pure. This is possible for us ; it is possible to live so near to God that nothing shall have power to disturb our peace, but amidst all the waves of this troublesome world we shall be unmoved. And this is what we have to do ; this is all that is worth living for. To know God, to fear Him, to serve Him, to dwell with Him ; here is the great end and aim of life. Then brethren recall the dealings of God with your souls, meditate upon His judgments with humble thoughtfulness, and with repentance for unfaithfulness, with fervent prayer for enlightenment and guidance in the way of truth. And may He who alone sees the end from the beginning, and who doeth all things well, give us wisdom and grace to acknowledge His hand in all things, and inspire us to that   *   *   *   *   *   *   *   *

[Here the MS. ends.   The conclusion was evidently intended to be extempore.]

THE END.